R MY NAME
IS RACHEL

ALSO BY PATRICIA REILLY GIFF

FOR MIDDLE-GRADE READERS

Storyteller

Wild Girl

Eleven

Water Street

Willow Run

A House of Tailors

Maggie's Door

Pictures of Hollis Woods

All the Way Home

Nory Ryan's Song

Lily's Crossing

The Gift of the Pirate Queen

The Casey, Tracey & Company books

FOR YOUNGER READERS

The Zigzag Kids books

The Kids of the Polk Street School books

The Friends and Amigos books

The Polka Dot Private Eye books

R MY NAME
IS RACHEL

PATRICIA REILLY GIFF

WENDY
LAMB
BOOKS

Text copyright © 2011 by Patricia Reilly Giff
Jacket art copyright © 2011 by Kamil Vojnar/Flying Blind Pictures

All rights reserved. Published in the United States by
Wendy Lamb Books, an imprint of
Random House Children's Books,
a division of Random House, Inc., New York.

Wendy Lamb Books and the colophon are trademarks
of Random House, Inc.

Visit us on the Web! www.randomhouse.com/kids

Educators and librarians, for a variety of teaching tools,
visit us at www.randomhouse.com/teachers

Library of Congress Cataloging-in-Publication Data
Giff, Patricia Reilly.
R my name is Rachel / by Patricia Reilly Giff. — 1st ed.
p. cm.
Summary: Three city siblings, now living on a farm during the Great Depression, must survive on their own when their father takes a construction job miles away.
ISBN 978-0-375-83889-7 (trade)—ISBN 978-0-375-93889-4 (lib. bdg.)—
ISBN 978-0-375-98389-4 (ebook)—ISBN 978-0-440-42176-4 (pbk.)
1. Depressions—1929—United States—Fiction. [1. Depressions—1929—
Fiction. 2. Brothers and sisters—Fiction. 3. Self-reliance—Fiction.
4. Farm life—Fiction. 5. Moving, Household—Fiction.] I. Title.
PZ7.G3626Raal 2011
[Fic]—dc19
2011004303

The text of this book is set in 12-point Goudy.

Book design by Kenneth Holcomb

Printed in the United States of America

10 9 8 7 6 5 4 3 2 1

First Edition

TO MY GRANDDAUGHTER
CHRISTINE ELIZABETH GIFF
WITH LOVE

LATE WINTER

CHAPTER ONE

I know my neighborhood by heart, so it wouldn't be hard to walk from our apartment to the stores blindfolded. And that's what I'm doing. Almost.

My book is up in front of my nose, hiding my face so no one will see the tears in my eyes. I'm almost at the end of the story and I'm sure Lad, the collie, is going to die. No matter that he's old, he's such a good dog.

But Lad isn't the only reason I'm trying not to cry. It's because of Pop, who right now is sitting in the big green chair in our living room.

Pop home, instead of working, on a winter afternoon! Pop without his job at the bank, and all because of the Depression.

"What does that mean?" I asked. And he said it's as if someone opened a plug and everyone's money went down the drain.

I know almost all our money is gone.

After lunch, when I was drying the dishes with him, I asked, "Can't you ask Uncle Elliot for help with money? Just until President Franklin Roosevelt fixes the Depression?"

"I'd never ask anyone for help," Pop says. "Not even my brother. Besides, he doesn't have any more money than I do."

"I guess I wouldn't ask for help either," I say, considering. All the heroes in the books I've read do it on their own, too.

Now I wipe my eyes with my sleeve and turn the corner to Charlie the Butcher's store. I press my nose against his window even though it's dusty and a leftover fly from last summer is spattered against the glass.

Charlie sees me and raps on the pane. Dum-de-de-dum-dum—

It means he has bologna, and he's going to give me a slice right off one end. My mouth waters, but I'm nervous. I want to ask him for two slices. I've never done that before. But Pop desperately needs cheering up. So this time it's crucial.

Crucial.

That's one of our words. Miss Mitzi Madden, of Madden's Blooms, and I are letter writers. We like to use important words on occasion.

I love that: *on occasion.*

I've thought about asking Charlie for a second slice of bologna all day. "It's just for this occasion," I'll say. And he'll say—

Who knows what he'll say?

I open the door, listening to the bell tinkle overhead. The sawdust on the floor crunches under my shoes as I go to the counter.

"Hello, dahling," Charlie says.

He says that to everyone.

"Is it possible on this occasion," I ask, "to have two slices of bologna?"

"Ah, good girl," he says. "You want to treat your sister, Cassie."

Not in a hundred years, but I don't say that. Instead, I glance at the pig's head in the case. Poor pig. His dead eyes stare up at me. The pig is the only thing in the case except for a shiny slab of liver and the bologna.

"It's because of the Depression," Pop explained to me the other day.

Everything has to do with the Depression. Pop, rail-thin, sitting in the sagging living room chair all week, his elbows on the windowsill, calls out once in a while: "There goes the mailman. I'm glad for him. Seven kids, he really needs his job," or "The milkman's trying to hold on, but no one can afford milk anymore."

It's because of the Depression, Pop says, that Mr. Appleby sells apples out of a barrel on Clinton Street; he polishes them with a rag so the buyers won't notice the brown spots. "Doesn't that just fit," my younger sister, Cassie, says. "Appleby selling apples?"

And what about me? All I want is a dog, or a cat, or even a fish in a tank that we can't afford.

Ridiculous. How much does one goldfish eat?

But Pop shakes his head. "No one has two nickels to rub together anymore."

Charlie slices the bologna paper-thin. "For such a good girl, Rachel, three slices." He beams at me, his teeth white under his mustache.

"I will never forget your generosity," I say. Then I add, "Don't forget the cat."

He pushes a fist-sized lump of meat toward me, grinning.

I pick up the lump with two fingers and the slices of bologna in their waxed paper jackets and skedaddle out of there. Outside, I deposit the lump under Clarence's tree, remembering the letter Miss Mitzi and I wrote to the governor. We told him a thing or two, mostly that we're very displeased about the Depression. Where did all the money and jobs go, anyway? I wonder if he's read it yet; I hope he takes it to heart.

Clarence is perched on a tree branch above my head. His red tail whips back and forth; his fierce eyes glare at me. He's waiting for me to leave so he can have his dinner.

I head for home, passing the schoolyard, and look up at my classroom window. Mrs. Lazarus says I soak up learning like a sponge. I smile to myself, imagining long division, the Civil War, and stories of the prairie schooners seeping right into my bones.

Down on the corner, I see my brother Joey's friend Paulie. He's standing over the sewer grate, holding . . .

Holding—

"Hey!" I start to run. Paulie grips Joey's pale ankles as Joey hangs upside down in the sewer.

"Pull him up right now," I say, "or I'll sock you in the breadbasket."

"Just a minute," Joey yells up.

"I'll give you a punch, too, Joey."

Paulie's breath is loud. It's not easy to hold someone over the sewer, even someone as skinny as Joey.

Joey yells, "Got it," and Paulie pulls him up until Joey grabs the curb with one filthy hand. With the other he raises a pole. A piece of chewed gum is stuck to the end. And stuck to the gum is—

"A penny," says Joey. His face is filthy, the dirt almost hiding the freckles that cover his nose.

"One day you'll fall in there and drown in that filth," I say.

Paulie bends over laughing, and I sweep past them, trembling, as I picture Joey's brown hair floating in muck.

He's only a year younger than I am; wouldn't you think he'd have more sense! We're steps and stairs, Pop says. Cassie's two years younger—she turned ten last month—and the bossiest kid on Colfax Street.

As I dash up the three flights of stairs to our apartment, I take a bite of bologna, because I just can't wait.

Right now Cassie is sitting at the kitchen table. Pop says we look almost like twins, except that I'm taller, and my hair's a little darker. Her feet are tucked under her, and a spoon dangles from her mouth. She turns it back and forth for the last taste of poor-man's rice pudding.

I lay the bologna slices out on the table, two perfect, one missing a small edge, like a jigsaw puzzle piece.

Cassie reaches out, but I yank the bologna away. "Sure, just like you saved some pudding for me. Oink."

"Oink yourself," she says.

"Girls, please," Pop calls from the living room.

I point to the slices. "One for me, one for Pop, and one for Miss Mitzi Madden of Madden's Blooms."

Cassie glares at me, but she knows Pop needs the bologna to cheer him up. And who can argue about Miss Mitzi? She's thin as a mop handle, but when she smiles, Pop says, the world lights up. Cassie and Joey love her as much as I do.

But then I feel guilty. I pass my jigsaw puzzle slice over to Cassie, who pushes it right back. "I don't need your germs, thank you," she says as Pop comes into the kitchen. But before I can offer him a slice, I see that his eyes look sad.

"What?" My voice is so low I can hardly hear it myself.

"We have to wait for Joey," he says.

We sit there, the three of us, the bologna almost forgotten, until Joey comes into the kitchen, whistling "Life Is Just a Bowl of Cherries."

Then Pop tells us the news.

It's devastating.

That's the worst word I can think of. But this is the worst news I can think of, too.

CHAPTER TWO

"I'll be back." My tear-filled voice floats out the door after me.

I have to tell Miss Mitzi Madden the news.

I fly down the stairs and rush along Colfax Street. My breath feels hard in my throat and I hold my hand on my side to cover the pain from running so fast.

It's almost time for Miss Mitzi to close Madden's Blooms and go upstairs to her apartment over the store.

Even though I don't have a moment to spare, I stop and bend over to catch my breath, to swipe at my eyes, to compose myself, as Miss Mitzi herself would say.

And then I'm in her shop, smelling the roses, and sweet peas, and feathery ferns lined up along her counter, and looking at Miss Mitzi, with her shiny dark hair and pink rouge on her cheeks.

"Ah, cupcake," she says with that light-up-the-world smile.

I go around the counter and reach out to her. She doesn't ask why. She wraps her arms around me and waits. I can't picture my own mother, who died too long ago for me to remember, but Miss Mitzi is certainly mother material.

And when I begin to talk, I don't even get to the heart of it, not yet. "All our plans," I say instead.

There's the letter we want to write to Admiral Byrd; we're both dying to know how it feels to fly over the South Pole with the polar bears lumbering around below. And we still haven't congratulated Babe Ruth, the baseball player, on hitting so many home runs.

But most of all, what about my secret plan for Pop to marry Miss Mitzi Madden?

After a while, Miss Mitzi walks me to the back of her shop. It's the best room in the world. The table that runs down the middle is filled with snippets of greens and silky petals, of ribbons and white doilies. There's always a pink flower, or a purple one, in a clear glass vase.

But not only that, on the small desk in the corner that's piled high with papers are the books Miss Mitzi and I read together in our spare time, our writing paper, our stamps, and the list of all the people we're going to write to.

Miss Mitzi goes to the front again to put the CLOSED, BUT I'D LOVE TO SEE YOU TOMORROW sign in her window. "Sit, Rachel," she says over her shoulder.

And I do that; I sink into her white rocker with the pale blue pillow. When she comes back, I open my mouth, ready to begin.

But Miss Mitzi holds up her hand. She fills the teakettle at the sink. "We'll have a cup together," she says. "Remember, everything feels better when you sip some sweet hot tea."

A moment later, I hold the cup in my hand, the warmth of it soothing me. Just opposite me, Miss Mitzi is perched on the edge of her table, her legs swinging a little. "Now," she says. "What could be so terrible?"

"We're leaving the city," I say.

I see her face. That's what's so terrible. She stands up and goes to the sink again to run water slowly over her hands, then dries her fingers one at a time. "Well," she says softly. It's almost a question.

"We're going to a faraway place called North Lake," I say. "Pop's heard of a bank job up there. A decent job. We'll take the last of our money and rent a small farm." I shrug. "It'll be less than our apartment rent."

"Chickens," she says absently. "A cow."

I hadn't thought about that. But what about Mrs. Lazarus, my teacher? What will she do without me soaking up learning? And what about all the letters Miss Mitzi and I were going to write? What about—

"What about you come with us?" I cross my fingers. I'd give up school, I'd give up everything, if only we had Miss Mitzi.

She turns from the sink and knocks over a pitcher of irises. The pitcher shatters, the flowers drift down and cover the floor like a purple carpet, and water spreads everywhere.

Miss Mitzi bends over and picks up a flower. She holds it to her cheek and I can see that she's crying.

Crying. Miss Mitzi.

"I'll ask Pop," I say. "Don't worry."

She lays an iris on the table and shakes her head. "Your father hasn't asked—" She breaks off and comes close to me. "What would this place do without my flowers? What would my few rich customers say if I deserted them?"

Her hands are wet from the broken vase and there's a small drop of blood on her finger.

"I don't care about the rich people," I say, and she probably doesn't care, either.

"I'll tell you what," she says. "We'll write back and forth. You'll tell me about the chickens and the cows. And I'll tell you about things down here."

I look up at the green clock on the wall. It's six-thirty; I'm supposed to be home for dinner.

"When are you leaving?" Miss Mitzi asks.

I raise one shoulder in the air. "Soon."

She nods. Then I go out through the front of the shop and start for home.

There's something else on my mind, something terrible, I know. But what it is, I can't remember.

I walk slowly now, pulling my coat collar up around my neck. It's cold and maybe it's going to rain. Or snow. A Model A Ford flashes by on the avenue, and lights dim in the few stores that are left.

I reach the front door of our apartment house, still wondering what I've forgotten.

And then I remember.

What will happen to Clarence, the cat, when I'm gone?

CHAPTER THREE

"Please let this work," I whisper as I climb the stairs.

Everyone is in the kitchen. Pop stands at the stove cracking soft-boiled eggs to go on top of baked potatoes. He puts his hand on my shoulder as I reach into the drawer next to him and pull out a few napkins. "Thanks, Rachel," he says.

Joey and Cassie sit at the table waiting. It's a wonder they don't have their mouths open like a pair of sparrows waiting to be fed. But I do the same thing; I slide onto my chair and wait until Pop sits. Then I tap my plate with the edge of my fork. "There's something we need to discuss."

Cassie's almost-nothing eyebrows disappear into her bangs. Joey frowns. He's worried I'm going to tell Pop that he knows more about the sewers than the sewer men.

I begin. "When we leave, Miss Mitzi will be all alone

at Madden's Blooms." I look at Pop, trying to let him see by my face how terrible that would be.

And he does see. He runs his hands through his thinning hair. "I've thought about that. I keep thinking about it."

"Suppose we bring her with us," I say.

"Great idea," Joey says around a mound of potato.

Pop's face is . . .

It's hard to tell how his face is. Serious? Worried? "That won't work, Rachel," he says.

But I can see that's what he wants to do. I just have to convince him. "We have to take her," I say desperately.

Pop leans forward. His voice sounds almost as desperate as mine. "I can't ask her to give up her shop—she's worked so hard—ask her to take us all on—" He breaks off and begins again. "Rachel, we don't have an extra cent. We don't know what kind of a place we're renting. All we know is what the real estate agent wrote. It's an old farmhouse with fields and a stream. There's no electricity right now; we'll have to heat the place with firewood."

"Sounds great," Joey says.

"Miss Mitzi would love it," I add.

Cassie pours a ton of salt on her dinner. "It could be falling apart. It might take a lot of work, especially since one of us does nothing but read and mess things up."

I want to reach across and pinch her freckled arm.

Pop ignores her. "Another thing," he says. "I know so little about the new job. Mr. Elmendorf, my old boss, said he'd fixed it up for me. I just have to be there two weeks from Monday."

"Please." I hold out my hands. I want some good news to take back to Miss Mitzi.

"Come on, Pop," Joey says.

Cassie bites her lip and stares down at the table. "Miss Mitzi would probably love to come with us."

At last, a little help from Cassie.

Pop reaches out. He takes my hand with one of his; he takes Cassie's with the other. If he had a third hand, it would be for Joey, he always says. "I wish there was a way to stay right here. It's your mother's place as well as Mitzi's. It's where I remember her."

I look around the kitchen. I forgot that Mom lived here. I struggle to remember her, but she died right after Cassie was born, so I was only a little more than two.

"So." Pop squeezes our hands. "We're taking a huge chance with the bank and a new place to live. But I farmed with my dad when I was a kid. I've missed the feel of the land. And there's nothing here for us."

"But, Pop—" Joey says.

Cassie has tears in her eyes and I open my mouth, but what else can I say? Then Pop stands up and walks by us, his hand sliding across my shoulder, his potato and egg uneaten on his plate.

I stand up next. "Thanks for trying," I say to Joey and Cassie. It's hard to get the words out. I go into the bedroom and throw myself on the bed.

An hour later, I remember that I haven't even

mentioned Clarence. Who's going to feed him if I'm not there to remind Charlie the Butcher? Clarence will simply have to live on birds and mice, a disgusting diet, and very sad for the birds and mice.

Poor Clarence. He's dirty, unfriendly, and sometimes mean. But who wouldn't be all those things if he was homeless and had one ear almost chewed off and one eye half closed?

In the bathroom I run a comb through my hair, which is straggly and knotted. I go down the hall and stop at the living room archway. Pop is sitting in his green armchair, staring down at the street.

"Pop, I'll do anything."

"Oh, honey," he says. "I have to have some pride. I can't ask her . . ."

His voice goes on, but I'm not listening. I go back into the bedroom without mentioning Clarence. I promise myself that I'll never give in on that. If Clarence can't come, I'll simply stay here. I'll live in the shed in back of the library and survive on bologna slices from Charlie the Butcher.

Later we troop outside, all of us except Cassie, who is ironing everything she owns to bring with her. Mr. Appleby stops at the curb on his way home from selling apples. We're looking at Pop's old truck, which will take us to North Lake.

"If it holds up," Joey whispers.

There are two seats in the closed-in cab, and the wide-open back is surrounded by wooden planks.

"The truck is—" Joey stops.

"The worst mess I've ever seen," I mutter. It's covered with a pale powdery dust; gray lumps litter the floor.

"My brother, Elliott, borrowed it for cement work," Pop tells Mr. Appleby. He reaches between the planks, grabs a soft clump, and crumbles it between his fingers.

Joey kicks at the back tire as if he's an expert. "She'll hold up till we get there, I guess."

"Of course," Mr. Appleby says.

"You kids can take turns sitting up front while two of you sit in back, plenty of room," Pop says.

My words slide out. "Clarence will have to sit in the front, too."

They turn to look at me. "Who's Clarence?" Pop asks.

I move away from the truck and stand with my legs apart, as if I'm facing a windstorm. "Clarence has fallen upon hard times." I read that in a book about an orphan and cried myself to sleep. "Clarence is a cat."

Everyone stares at me.

"We can't afford—" Pop begins.

"I love cats," says Joey.

And dear Mr. Appleby says, "Nothing like a cat in a barn to chase away the rodents."

I look from Joey to Pop.

"I guess," Pop says, sounding doubtful. "We had barn cats when I was growing up."

Joey taps his fingers on the truck's wooden railing. "Hope no one falls out."

"We'll hold on to each other." I know I've won a victory. The problem will be getting Clarence from his tree to the truck, but I'll face that on moving day.

CHAPTER FOUR

In my pajamas, I raise my bedroom window, which faces the brick wall of the next building, and angle my head into that thin space outside. It's freezing and the wind tears at my hair. Stars appear, then disappear between shreds of rushing clouds. I choose the brightest speck of gold and pretend it's the planet Pluto, even though I know Pluto is too far out to see.

I think of Pluto as mine. Why not? It was discovered on my birthday a few years ago. Miss Mitzi and I even sent in a name for it, Diana, much better than Pluto.

I slide into bed. Cassie always hogs three-quarters of it. "You're digging your elbows into my back," I tell her.

"Excuse me for breathing."

"Stay on your own side, if you don't mind." I pull my feet out of the covers and walk them up the wall.

"That's a foul habit," she says, but I know her eyes are drooping; she's half-asleep. "You've made footprints all over the place, and big toe marks. I can hardly stand to look at them."

I'm impressed that she knows the word *foul*. It's a word Miss Mitzi and I might use.

"What are people going to think of us?" Cassie asks.

She's losing her mind. "How many people parade through our bedroom?" I can almost stretch my arms from one side of this cubby of a room to the other. I peer at the blank brick wall across the way. "Maybe you think someone's staring in at us."

"What about the people who'll rent after us?" Cassie says. "I hope I don't get blamed for this mess."

"Who cares what anyone thinks?" I wave my foot in a perfect circle.

Cassie can be such a pest. I do remember, though, what Miss Mitzi said once. She was arranging flowers in a vase: pink carnations, white daisies, and one orange rose.

"Does that orange one belong in there?" I asked.

"You know what I found out?" Miss Mitzi tilted her head. "Everything doesn't have to go together exactly. It's more fun when something doesn't quite match." And then she added so softly that I wasn't sure I'd heard her right, "Like you and Cassie. Two different spirits."

Cassie is definitely an orange something or other. I turn to another worry. What will the new school in North Lake be like? And will the new teacher be a fountain of information, like Mrs. Lazarus? I think about my old friends

Peggy and Mary. Both of them moved away this year, too, because of the Depression.

But that's the last I remember until morning.

I spend the next week gathering everything in a box so I can remember this place forever. Too bad it's winter. I could have taken a leaf from a ginkgo tree. Under my bed I find an old bottle filled to the brim with sand and shells from Coney Island. I dust it off and put it in the box.

I go downstairs and through the alley to scoop up a spoonful of Colfax Street dirt—not easy, because it's hard as cement. Still, I manage. I tie the dirt up in my old slip, and that goes in next.

I add my first lost tooth—pale and cracked—twenty-five cents, a stamp, and an old bottle of Shalimar perfume, which Pop gave me. "It belonged to your mother," he said.

There's a trace of dried brown perfume in the bottom, which I breathe in sometimes. When I do that, I almost remember her.

CHAPTER FIVE

On the next Tuesday, I'm awake first. Last night I said goodbye to Miss Mitzi. I reach up and touch the locket she clasped around my neck. There's a tiny picture of the two of us on one side and a pressed piece of fern on the other. "Ferns look delicate, but they're strong," she told me. "Just like our friendship."

She gave me a second locket for Cassie and a fishing rod for Joey. "Don't forget me," she says, her sky-blue eyes filled with tears.

How could I ever forget her?

"I'll tell Pop you said that, too," I say.

She doesn't answer; she just shakes her head.

Now I climb over Cassie, throw on my clothes, and go into the kitchen.

Pale light streams through the dusty window, and the bricks on the opposite building have lost their usual angry look. They're soft and rosy; it's a perfect late-winter day.

I begin to search. Nothing is left in the icebox, nothing in the cabinets. Everything's been cleaned for the move. Cassie spent hours last night washing the shelves and scrubbing the floor with borax and a brush.

I rustle through the garbage bag and come up with three stringy carrots and a sad-looking spear of broccoli. Like me, Clarence is a meat eater. He wouldn't even look at this wilted mess.

Charlie the Butcher won't open his door one minute before nine a.m. He runs his life according to the clock. Pushing back the straw hat he wears winter and summer, he goes through his schedule, from six, when he awakes, until ten, when he gets back into bed: the most boring schedule in the world.

But there it is. We have to get on the road before eight. And how am I ever going to capture Clarence without food?

It's impossible to scoop him up. Clarence has allowed me to touch him only once, and that was because my fingers were smeared with fat from Charlie's stew meat.

Never mind. I let myself out of the apartment and fly down the stairs, playing A My Name Is Alice and My Husband's Name Is Albert as my feet meet each step. It's a comforting game, because all I have to concentrate on is the alphabet. We come from Alabama and we sell . . .

The choices are endless. Apples, abalones, accordions, acorns—

I stop at school for a last look up at my classroom. And

there's Mrs. Lazarus at the window. I wave at her and she opens the window to poke her head out.

"Rachel, I'll miss you," she calls.

I feel a thickness in my throat. "I'll miss you, too. But don't worry. I'll still learn, even in North Lake."

"I know you will," she says.

By the time I reach Charlie's corner, I'm up to R my name is Rachel. Clarence stares at me balefully from the lowest branch of the sycamore. *Balefully*, a perfect word.

"Here, kitty, kitty," I say in a tender voice.

Clarence closes his one good eye and turns his head away as I shinny up the trunk, grabbing his branch.

He rakes my wrist with his claw, but I pay no attention. I reach out with one hand, and he leaps higher, to the next branch.

I follow him. It's like playing leapfrog. I jump; he jumps.

It's impossible.

"If only you knew what you're missing," I call. "You could be on a farm with a barn full of hay and a stream full of fish. And if you stay here, Charlie will forget you some days, you'll be hungry and sad. . . ."

I slide back on a branch to lean against the tree trunk. I don't know what to do. I'm really at my wit's end.

Those are Mrs. Lazarus's words when she tries to make Edward Ray do what he's supposed to.

"Oh, Clarence." I know I'll have to give up.

I hear footsteps below me. I look down, wondering who it is. Cassie is coming toward me.

Something white billows over her shoulder. And is

that my cereal bowl she's carrying? She sees me and stops. She does that Jell-O thing, squishing her cheeks back and forth.

"What are you doing?" she says. "Everyone is waiting."

I don't want to talk to her, so I close my eyes, pretending she's not there. I hear her, though. Is she shinnying up the tree? Yes. That's exactly what she's doing.

I open one eye, expecting Clarence to claw his way to another branch. But she holds out my bowl and he edges his way toward her.

I can't believe it. Cassie is doing me a favor.

She sits on the branch and watches while Clarence eats whatever she's brought for him. Where did she even find something in that empty kitchen?

Like lightning, she opens a pillowcase. With Clarence spitting and hissing, she wrestles it over his back end and he drops inside like an apple plucked from a tree. The bowl flies off the branch and breaks, Cassie loses her balance, and the two fall to the ground, the pillowcase writhing. Cassie screeches, "I'm dead."

I come down from the tree. Gingerly I pick up the pillowcase; I hold it out in front of me as Cassie gets up and dusts herself off.

I don't say thank you; I'm speechless. But she has to know I'm grateful. I'm going to do something nice for her the first chance I get. How did she even know I had a cat?

Without a word, we hurry back to the apartment. Outside, Pop and Joey are tying a dresser to the back of the truck.

The truck is packed tightly with our clothes, the rosewood rocking chair, and our enormous trunk. Besides the picnic basket, which is filled with sandwiches for lunch.

But best of all, besides the locket, are the presents I've gotten, which I've tucked in with my mementos: an apple from Mr. Appleby, a card from Charlie that's greasy and smells like the butcher shop, and a book from Mrs. Lazarus, *Rebecca of Sunnybrook Farm*.

I can't believe it. I actually own a book. When we get to the farm, I'll read it. I'll go through it as slowly as I can to make it last.

"I have to sit in the front for a while," I tell everyone, and gesture to the pillowcase, which has calmed down a little. "The cat will have to be inside."

Pop nods and Joey boosts himself up the side of the truck and plunks himself down in the rocker.

"Wait a minute." Cassie's hands are on her hips. "I'm sitting in front with the cat."

I close my eyes. That Cassie. But her dress is ripped, and she has a jagged scratch along her cheek, all because of Clarence. All because of me.

"All right," I say through clenched teeth, and add, "For now."

"Take turns, girls," Pop says over his shoulder.

Through the pillowcase, I whisper to Clarence, "It's all for the best," then I hold it out to Cassie.

"Well, Leo," Pop says to Mr. Appleby. "This is it."

Mr. Appleby reaches out to shake Pop's hand; he turns to the rest of us and shakes our hands, too. "Don't worry about anything," he says. "Look forward, not back."

As Pop starts up the truck, I climb in next to Joey.

Through the cab window I see Cassie open the pillowcase. Clarence comes out, biting and hissing, and dives under the seat.

I take a last glance at the apartment house, the only place I've lived since I was born. "Goodbye, old friend," I whisper. As we turn the corner, I glance up at a sky so blue it almost hurts my eyes. A few clouds, like torn paper, drift along.

I've been up forever today, so I pull the old quilt around me and close my eyes. When I open them later, I see fields with bare trees and patches of snow.

For the first time, I really wonder about the farm. Will there be a red barn with a cow already there, waiting for us? Or maybe there'll be a wishing well in front and a porch with rockers on the side.

Joey's hair is blown back against his ears; he holds up one hand to catch the wind. "Great practice," he says.

What is he talking about? Then I remind myself that he wants to be a flagpole sitter, like Shipwreck Kelly, when he grows up. It's an appalling goal, especially because Shipwreck sits on poles for days and they have to lift up a tent on pulleys so he can go to the bathroom in privacy. It makes me shudder.

Moments later, we see a field filled with huge boxes leaning against each other. Some are made of wood, others of cardboard that buckles here and there. A man stands in front of one with his pockets turned inside out.

"Are people living in those things?" I ask.

"Pop told me there are places like this all over the country, Hoovervilles, for the homeless." Joey points to the man. "See his empty pockets hanging out? Hoover flags. He's telling the world that President Hoover didn't do a thing to stop this Depression."

I nod, remembering that Pop is counting on President Roosevelt to fix things up. At least Pop's pockets aren't empty. And even though we're leaving the city, we'll still have a home somewhere.

There are more fields as we go on, but they're rich and brown, with almost no snow; they're waiting for spring planting, I guess. And then I see my first cow, her black-and-white face wide and peaceful.

But how will we manage with this new farm? Last night Pop's face was serious. "Once we plunk the rent money down, that'll be that. We'll have to make it work. All of us. Together."

Don't look back, I tell myself. Look forward, Rachel.

CHAPTER SIX

North Lake is a bowl scooped out of the mountains. Cutting it exactly in half is Front Street, with its bank, and its post office, and a few stores. All of it is thick with snow.

Across the way a train pulls out of the station, puffing steam. We watch three men dart across the street and run along next to the train. Two of them hop on, but when the third one misses, he throws himself on the ground, pounding his fists.

"Hobos moving from one place to another, looking for work," Pop says as he gets out of the truck. He goes into the real estate office and talks to a man, who gives him a key; the man waves his arms around, probably giving him directions to the farm.

We drive along roads, going right and left and right, zigzagging along, passing barns and houses that are falling apart. And then, somehow, we're back in town. Lost.

We start again. Joey and I look at each other. We're sick of this trip, tired of being poked by the rocking chair, which shifts when we go uphill. Joey opens the picnic basket and we dive in, eating egg salad sandwiches washed down with watery lemonade.

It's much colder now; trees stand out black against the sky, although a fine mist of snow is beginning to fall. I'm shivering and my teeth begin to chatter. Joey knocks on the cab window. "Give Rachel a turn in there. She's freezing."

Pop pulls over to the side.

"What about you?" I ask Joey.

"I'm fine," he says. But he isn't fine. He's as cold as I am. Still, I change places with Cassie, taking a sandwich for Pop.

Along the road we pass a house with a sign in front: DR. NICOLS AT YOUR SERVICE. Farther down is a farm with a white fence that needs painting. There's a sign, too: GET YOUR GOAT. TWENTY-FIVE CENTS. Someone has drawn a small cup and saucer on the bottom of the fence.

"Odd," I say.

"A hobo drew that," Pop says. "He wanted to say that the owners will give anyone who needs it a cup of coffee."

Next there's the quickest flash of a school. I swivel around to get a look, but then it's gone.

A wind has come up; it pushes against the truck, the sound of it lonely, as if we're lost in the snow and ice of the Arctic.

At last we turn in and bump down a rutted road just big enough for the truck. At the end is a farm. The barn isn't red; it's gray with missing boards; slices of a white field show through on the sides. There certainly won't be a cow in there all by herself.

The house is worse. Paint peels off in great strips, and the shutters, which must have been blue once, are faded and hang at crazy angles.

Pop brakes a foot away from the porch. Some porch! The railing is falling off. Stacks of wood are thrown every which way.

I look back at the path Pop's created in the snow. "It was too cold to walk through that old cornfield," he says. He rests his head on the wheel as I hold out the sandwich. He shakes his head. "I'm not hungry."

But Clarence is willing to forget how angry he is for a bite. He moves out from under the seat, peering up at me with his good eye.

I tear off a piece, and as he eats, I touch his rough head, then run my hand down his knobby back. He's thin and dirty and his fur is matted. But I've learned something about him. He's willing to tolerate me if I feed him.

Tolerate. Miss Mitzi would love that word.

Pop squints at the house. "The agent said there's plenty of wood for the fireplace." He grins at me. "Never mind. Next week when I'm working, we'll be able to get the electricity up and running."

"We could still go back home," I say. I'd go straight to Madden's Blooms. Miss Mitzi and I would lock arms and dance around her icebox the way we did when President Roosevelt was elected. We sang "Happy Days Are Here Again" at the tops of our voices.

But I remind myself that Clarence's only hope is a barn with a bed of hay, and a stream with tiny silver fish for dinner. And Pop shakes his head. "People are moving into our apartment today." He reaches out to snare the last bit of sandwich. "Sorry, cat," he says absently.

Cassie and Joey climb over the back of the truck. They stand next to Pop's open window, hunched against the wind. "This is it?" Cassie says; her eyes fill.

I feel sorry for her; I feel sorry for all of us. And I've had to go to the bathroom for hours. "Bathroom."

"Outhouse," Pop says.

I shove the truck door open; I have to push hard against the wind. There are pins and needles in both my feet, so I slide out and land in a heap in the snow. Behind me, Clarence dives out. He streaks around the side of the house into the woods and he's gone.

Gone.

"Come back!" I call. "Come back, cat!"

"What have you done?" Cassie is almost screaming as she runs toward the woods.

We watch her. I know it's no use. Clarence is much too fast. Suppose he never comes back. I picture him lost in this lonely place. I keep calling, my voice sounding high and thin against the wind.

Pop points us to the outhouse: a shed with a half-moon cutout over the door. Imagine going to the bathroom outdoors.

Cassie comes back, her face swollen. Then we stand in line as if we're in school, heads tucked into our coats. When it's my turn, I go inside and shut the door. Lacy cobwebs soften the corners, but the spiders that crocheted them are gone; the winter must have been too cold for them.

As I open the door to leave, what's left of the light comes in against the wall. Someone's drawn something there with crayons. It's a cat, not unlike Clarence with his rough fur and threadlike whiskers. Once a family lived here, and maybe a girl like me had drawn it.

But it's too cold to stand there staring at the drawing; besides, Joey is waiting. I go up the steps of the house with Pop and Cassie, looking over my shoulder, calling, "Cat, here, cat!"

"A lot of good that will do," Cassie says.

Joey comes after us. Our feet are loud against the porch floor; our voices echo as we open the unlocked door.

On one side of the hall is a living room; on the other side are stairs, which climb to the second floor, and a kitchen larger than any I ever saw at home. There's furniture here and there: a couch and an armchair like Pop's old one in the living room, a long table and painted chairs in the kitchen.

It's too dark to go upstairs, too scary. Pop goes out on the porch and brings in an armful of wood, which he stacks in the living room fireplace and lights with matches he's found on the mantel. "The wood is damp," he says. "It will take time to catch."

We watch until at last a thin curl of smoke wends its way upward. Then Pop and Joey go out to the truck and come back with all our things: the rocking chair, boxes, blankets, and pillows, and the bags of food Cassie packed.

We spread out on the living room floor in a row, munching on crackers and cheese.

We're all so tired that it doesn't make any difference that it's only six-thirty or seven o'clock. Somewhere a shutter bangs against the house, but we're close enough to reach out to each other. We've never had a fireplace before; I watch the flames and feel their warmth as I slide down into the blankets. If only Clarence were here.

Pop says, "Don't worry. I'm going to work. We'll be able to buy things when I get paid. You'll see. In the end, we'll love this place."

"Really," Cassie says as if she doesn't believe it.

I don't believe it either, and I wonder if Pop does.

But that's my last thought until a thin light spreads itself across the bare floor.

It's morning.

Dear Miss Mitzi,

Clarence is gone. I feel as if my heart is broken.

I remember you told me you had a cat once named Lazy who was lost. He came home, didn't he?

I know you said you'd like to live on a farm. You'd plant a peach tree and grow roses on a white trellis.

I told Pop. He said he could picture you doing that, but he couldn't imagine asking you to live in a house in this condition.

Some condition. There are holes in the roof.

Love from your friend forever,
Rachel

CHAPTER SEVEN

At the kitchen table, I tuck my letter to Miss Mitzi into my pocket. Then I tiptoe down the hall. Everyone is still asleep under coats and blankets. Cassie's curls cover her face, Joey's mouth is open and his arms are spread wide, and Pop snores gently on the end. I'm still wearing yesterday's dress, two sweaters, socks that have holes in both toes, and a jacket. My wool hat is pulled down over my forehead.

The light is strange this morning; something covers the windows. And then I realize it's snow. The last time it snowed at home, there was only enough on the ground to make footprints along the avenue before it melted. I wonder if there will be more than that here.

I tiptoe into the hall and look up. At the top of the

stairs is a round stained-glass window. Even though snow lies over it like a blanket, I still see the pink and purple and orange. Miss Mitzi colors.

Running my hands along the walls, I go up the stairs, steps creaking. At the end of the hall is another window. I go toward it, hoping to spot Clarence somewhere out back. The window is encrusted in snow; I blow on it and make a small clear circle. What I see is shocking.

Outside, the world is gray; wind blows the falling snow sideways. It must have been snowing all night. I have a quick panicky feeling. How will we ever get out of here?

And what about going to the new school? I dreamed about the glimpse I had of it on the way here. It was a happy dream.

How could Clarence ever survive this? If he had so far, he must be terrified that he's suddenly in a strange place, away from his tree and the butcher shop around the corner. It's hard to catch my breath, but I remember something Miss Mitzi said once: *You can think of only one thing at a time. Choose wisely.*

I hold my locket between my fingers as I walk along the hall, counting: four bedrooms, three with bare mattresses dotted with mouse dirt. Horrible. The last one is empty, no furniture at all. I step inside. The walls are covered with drawings of cats and kittens and a duck that waddles up toward the ceiling. Once this room must have been perfect, and so was the girl who drew the animals. I wish I'd known her. I twirl around looking at the pictures.

I might even love sleeping in this room with those kittens and ducks smiling down at me.

Out in the hall again, I push open another door. It's a staircase with drawings on the wall all the way down: a stream with rocks like turtle backs, and willow trees dipping their branches in for a drink.

At the bottom there's a box of chalk with some of the colors missing. The girl must have forgotten them when she left. I push open the door and I'm in the kitchen.

Cassie stands there, frowning. "Why are you lurking around in the closet?"

Lurking!

I try to remember that she saved Clarence yesterday. Only yesterday? "It's a secret staircase," I tell her, even though I should keep it to myself. Why should I share it with such a miserable girl?

Pop comes to the doorway, combing his hair with his fingers, and hugs us. "Snow," he says, not really paying attention to it. I know he's worried about us and how cold we must be, standing there in that icy kitchen in coats and hats, with scarves slung around our necks.

But on one wall there's a fireplace, big enough to stand in; the wood inside is barely singed. Pop crouches on the floor and gets a fire going. In no time, the flames roar out at us, making me almost breathless with their warmth. If only I could find Clarence. He'd love sleeping by the fire, his tail wrapped around him.

Cassie pushes curtains back from the ice-covered window. "The snow is really piling up out there."

Cassie loves snow. When it storms at home, she opens the window and scoops up a handful, working it into a ball. She's the first one out the door to catch snowflakes in her mismatched mittens.

Joey comes out of the living room, stretching, laughing. He goes straight to the window and rubs it with his sleeve. "Look at that snow. I think we're going to be lucky here."

Pop smiles at him. "Joey, you keep us all going."

"Listen, Pop," he says. "Did you see the weather vane up on the roof? It's a rooster. Funny-looking thing with his head back as if he's crowing." He chews on his lip. "All I'd have to do is shinny up there and polish it up. It'll look like a million dollars."

"You'd be like Shipwreck Kelly sitting on a flagpole," Cassie says.

I feel my heart turn over. I can almost see him climbing up on the roof, then sliding down, leaving a clear path in the snow behind him.

We all stand at the window then, listening to the glass rattling in the wind; icy air blows in around the edges.

"I can't believe it," Pop says. "How deep must that be?" He runs his hand along the sill. "Maybe we can put some newspaper here if we find any. One thing about snow—it will cover some of the chinks in the walls."

He glances up at the kitchen ceiling, a frown line appearing between his eyebrows. "It won't help the holes in the roof," he says. And even now I see a dusting of snow on the floor.

What a strange world it is outside. Along the edge of the field, tree branches are heavy with inches of snow. White flakes swirl in the gray sky, and wind pushes them into huge drifts.

"Poor cat," Cassie says. "Poor, poor cat." She glares at me.

Pop goes to the bags on the counter and starts to line up things for breakfast. We sit hunched at the long table someone left, shedding our coats and then our sweaters while Pop cuts the bacon. He lights a match, and the stove top lets off an orange-blue flame. The bacon curls and fries as he drops eggs into a spider pan we brought with us.

"Eggs, bacon, toasted bread . . ." He hesitates. "And sweet hot tea."

I look at him quickly. I'm sure he's thinking about Miss Mitzi. He turns away, though, before I can see his face.

My mouth waters as the bacon twists in the pan and the eggs turn brown around the edges. I've never smelled anything so good. Maybe steam from the bacon will waft through the holes in the roof. Cats are supposed to have a terrific sense of smell, and that might bring Clarence out of hiding.

"When my father was a boy," Pop says, "there was a terrible snowstorm along the East Coast, the blizzard of 1888. That was in March, too. His grandmother brought the chickens into the kitchen from the barn. They didn't get out of the house for days—" He breaks off. "I have to go to town tomorrow," he says at last. "No matter what. I have to get that job at the bank."

We're all silent, staring out the window. The truck must be covered with snow, of course.

How will Pop ever get out of here?

And what will happen if he can't?

How did we get so far away from home?

One thought at a time. Choose wisely.

CHAPTER EIGHT

In the late afternoon, the light is dim; it will be dark soon. Still it doesn't stop snowing. Pop has been carrying wood inside for hours and cleaning the fireplace in the living room. He's curled up on an old sofa now, wrapped in his coat, sound asleep. Cassie and Joey are upstairs; I hear them talking back and forth.

I have to get outside and search for Clarence. Who knows what I did with my galoshes? I yank on Joey's and stuff them with old newspaper. Already his feet are bigger than mine.

I can't get out the back door. Snow has sealed it shut. In the front hall, I can barely hold on to the door as it opens into the wind. It swings back, but surprisingly, there's almost no snow on the porch. The wind has whooshed it away. I tell myself I'm a pioneer, like Laura in *Little House in the Big Woods*.

I start down the steps and sink past my knees into an icy-cold drift. I try to take another step, and realize I've lost one of Joey's galoshes. I can't go forward; I can't even get back on the porch. I call out, but no one answers.

I begin to cry, the tears warm on my cheeks. I yell then—it's an angry screech—and at last Pop swings open the door.

"My dear Rachel." He lifts me out of the snow and helps me into the house, holding me. We rock back and forth in the hall, his heavy shirt warm against my cheek. He whispers, "I'm sorry. I'm so sorry."

"How will I ever get to school?" I say through my tears.

For a moment, he's completely silent. "I've been meaning to tell you . . ."

I lean back so I can see his face. He looks sadder than I've ever seen him before.

"The real estate man told me the school is closed." Pop shakes his head. "He says they'll get it going again soon. They have no money to pay the teachers now."

Joey stands at the end of the hall. No school is good news for him. Cassie is right behind him, picking at her fingernail. Who knows what she's thinking?

I picture a sponge that's dry; it shrivels up into almost nothing. I'm that sponge. "What about the library?"

Pop doesn't answer.

That means the library is closed. How can that be? I can't even cry. No library: the idea is too big for tears.

"This depression can't last forever," Pop says. "And when it's over, things will go back to normal. School will open; so will the library. You'll see, Rachel. You have to believe that."

I shrug out of my coat and unwind my scarf. "One of your galoshes is out there, under the snow," I tell Joey, my voice not steady. "I'll get it back for you as soon as the snow begins to melt."

Will it ever melt?

Joey waves his hand in the air. "Don't worry. There are boots piled up in a pantry closet."

Only one thing at a time.

"Do you mind if I take the bedroom with the cat pictures?" I aim the question at Cassie. No one else will care. My voice sounds strange, almost as if it doesn't make any difference what she says.

She squints at me. "Which room is that?"

"The smallest. In back."

She tilts her head. "Go ahead," she says at last.

I start up the stairs.

"Rachel," Pop and Joey say almost at the same time.

"I'm all right," I say.

I go into the bedroom and sit against the wall.

Oh, Clarence.

I put my things around me, rattling my bottle of sand and shells from Coney Island; I sniff the empty bottle of Shalimar perfume, read Charlie the Butcher's greasy card, then pull out my Rebecca book.

It's satisfyingly thick. I know I have to spread out the reading to make it last, but today I'll read two pages instead of the one I promised myself. Maybe even three pages.

The idea is as soothing as sweet hot tea.

* * *

It's almost dark when the snow stops. From the window, I can see that a dusty moon glimmers overhead. I haven't read three pages; I've read fifty-three. I have to slow down.

I kneel up to watch the field. I wonder about my old friends from school, Peggy and Mary, who moved away because of the Depression. Could they be in a strange place, the way we are?

I keep looking outside. If I see Clarence tunneling through the snow, can I even go out and help him? But what I see is almost a miracle. Snow has drifted away from the fence on the side of the field. It's almost bare, with tan weeds showing their heads. I could walk carefully all the way to the back.

Downstairs, I find the boots Joey was talking about and head out. The wind sweeps across the field, sending veils of snow into the air. Beyond that is a blur of trees. I wade toward them, looking up at the few stars that have come out. The planet Pluto is up there, looking down at me.

In a few more steps, I'm at the barn. The door is open. Is it possible that Clarence is hidden in there somewhere? I step inside. It takes me a moment to get used to the half dark. But then I look at the stalls, which must have sheltered cows once. I reach down and pick up a bit of the hay that's in piles, and over my head I see the loft. An old lantern hangs from a hook on the stairs to that loft.

This is a place to nestle in the hay and read, a place for a cow, for a goat, for chickens.

I spin around, my arms out, the way I did in that bedroom. I feel something in my chest, something I couldn't have imagined a few minutes ago. It's a bit of happiness taking over a small edge of my heart—in spite of everything.

But Clarence isn't here. I go outside again. A rusty chicken wire fence pokes up through the snow. It bends with me as I try to climb it, so I just stand there, shivering, calling, "Clarence, please come back!"

The wind tears the words away from me, and I know he can't hear me. How can he with half an ear torn off? Still I keep shouting for him.

"You don't belong here," a voice says, and I spin around. I don't see anyone at first, just a shape in snowshoes in the next field. "Go home where you belong!" he yells.

I squint to see better. It's a boy wearing an old hat, hunched up in his jacket.

I take a step back, but then I open my mouth. Miss Mitzi always says manners help in a pinch. "Have you seen my cat?" I ask nicely. "He's quite—"

I hesitate. What's a word that will bring sympathy to that awful boy? I clear my throat. "He's quite fragile."

The boy begins to laugh. "I knew it. You don't know a thing about the country. Someone saw a bear with her cub the other day, and there are mountain lions and coyotes." He leers at me. "Do you know what they eat?"

Cats? Could he be telling the truth?

He's still talking. "And a skinny city thing like you. Gone in a gulp."

Suddenly I'm filled with anger so fierce I can hardly

believe it. It's the last straw. Leaving home to come to this place with no light, no heat, no school, no library.

No nothing.

"Don't you dare!"

He laughs again, pointing at me. "What are you going to do about it?"

Never mind Miss Mitzi and her manners.

I crouch down to scoop up a clump of snow. "I come from the city," I tell him in my fiercest voice. "And you know what they say?"

"Who cares?" He's still laughing.

"They say we're born wearing boxing gloves." I crunch the snow between my freezing hands and let go. My aim is deadly from years of stickball on Colfax Street, but he steps sideways just in time. He stands there, mouth open in surprise.

I tuck my chin deep into my scarf just in case he intends to fight back, and bend over for another scoop. But he's laughing; he turns and trudges away from me along the fence line.

"Round one!" I yell after him, but the anger is draining away. What would Miss Mitzi say?

"Clarence!" I call a few more times, and then go back to the house, remembering what Mrs. Lazarus used to tell Edward Ray: *I'm mortified at your behavior.*

Dear Miss Mitzi,

You can't imagine how much snow we have. I will mail my two letters to you as soon as I can get them to the mailbox at the end of the road. It's probably rusty, but I'll clean it out as soon as I can.

Our address is Waltz Road. That's a musical name, isn't it?

I hope you write to me soon. I want to know about Lazy, your cat from years ago. Clarence hasn't found us yet.

Please don't tell Charlie the Butcher that Clarence has disappeared. He'll be heartsick at the news.

I miss you and Madden's Blooms. I miss the smell of lilies and the cold air when you open the icebox door.

Love,
Rachel

CHAPTER NINE

Pop is up early this morning, wearing his gray suit and a silky red tie with dots. He grins at us. "How do I look?"

"You could be the president," I say.

He runs his hand over my head, then pulls on his coat and goes outside with shovels he's found in the cellar.

The three of us go after him to help as much as we can. The snow is heavy, but once we clean the truck off, Pop will be set to go to town for his first day at the bank.

We use our mittens and sleeves to clean off the windows. "Still early." Pop is smiling again. "Plenty of time."

The bottoms of his trousers are soaked; his shoes must be, too. But he swings into the truck and we stand back as he starts it up. He crunches back and forth for a few minutes and we hold our breath. But then he backs out toward the road and I put my face up to the sun, which is warm on my cheeks. "It's a new day," I say.

"I'm going to get up there on the roof as soon as it gets a little warmer," Joey says. "While I work on the rooster, I bet I'll be able to see for forty miles."

I shiver and Cassie says, "You'll kill yourself up there. Won't that be the last straw!"

And somehow the three of us are laughing. Joey clumps up a snowball and tosses it at her, deliberately missing, and we troop into the kitchen, where the fireplace is blazing.

The three of us sink down at the table and chew on toast that has gotten a little cold but is still delicious, with lumps of butter here and there. We sip at tea, no longer hot but still sweet.

"I always wanted a pet," Cassie says. "Maybe we'll have chickens, and how about a goat? Remember that sign: 'Get Your Goat . . . Twenty-Five Cents'?"

I wonder at that. Cassie wants a pet, too. I think of Miss Mitzi putting an orange flower in with the pinks and purples. Strange. Cassie's definitely that orange flower, but maybe not quite as orange as I thought.

She has to spoil it. "We'll have to clean up in here, Rachel. I can't stand your crumbs all over the place."

"My crumbs? Mine?" I push back from the table and sweep the crumbs into my cupped hand. Three crumbs! Then I go upstairs to my Rebecca book. I'll read only one page. Only one. But it's so hard to do.

How terrible it would be not to have anything to read. I'd have to read *Rebecca* over and over, like someone on a desert island waiting for rescue. I pretend that I'm somewhere like that; I can bring only four things with me. What would they be? Books, for a start. So three more.

I could spend hours figuring that out. Days, even.

I guess I'd have to bring Pop, Miss Mitzi, Joey . . . and that's four. I grin to myself. *Too bad, Cassie, you'd have to stay home!*

When I've read ten more pages—ten—I hear the front door open and footsteps come into the hall. I go to the top of the stairs. Pop is back. Back already?

I follow him into the kitchen as he slides into the empty chair at the end of the table. He's soaking wet.

"The plow came through," he says, "but it piled snow up at the side of the road. There was no way I could get out in the truck. I tried to walk." He spreads his hands wide and shakes his head. "It must be three miles; I just couldn't do it."

"They'll understand at the bank," Joey says. "The weather is still terrible."

I jump in. "Don't worry, maybe the bank isn't even open this morning."

Pop nods. "I'll change into work clothes and we'll begin to clean the bedrooms."

And that's what we do. We begin with mine, even sweeping in the corners, washing the insides of the windows, then look at each other. What will we do for a bed in here?

"There are two beds in my room," Joey says. "You can have one."

We take one of the mattresses and drag it down the

stairs and out onto the porch. Not an easy trip, because Cassie is moaning the whole time that we're leaving mouse dirt on every step.

But how satisfying it is when we pound the mattress with the beaters we found in the pantry. We pound until the dust flies and we're all coughing, but somehow I begin to sing "Happy Days Are Here Again," and everyone joins in.

I sing as loud as I can, to attract Clarence and, just in case that mountain lion boy is around, to let the boy know he doesn't bother me one bit.

Dear Miss Mitzi,

I have disastrous news. Pop will not be working at the bank. By the time he got there late in the afternoon, his job was taken.

I'm writing to President Roosevelt to tell him to hurry up and get this depression over with. He's been in office since March 4, and March is almost over.

Pop leaves early every morning, driving from one town to another, to find work. He comes back after dark looking so cold. He stands in front of the fireplace in the kitchen, his hands out to catch the heat; his boots drip, leaving icy patches on the floor. But then he shakes himself and begins to get the house fixed up. One night he washed down the hall walls. Another night he got up on a ladder and plastered the ceiling. I heard him whistling a little.

But soon he won't have any gas left in the truck. I

wonder how he'll look for work. What will he do then? What will we all do?

A million cobwebs were in the mailbox out by the road, but no spiders. Maybe they moved into the house as soon as it got cold. Can't you see it? A line of little gray spiders—each one carrying a suitcase in a skinny feeler, holding a hat on with another—slides under the door and down the hall to the kitchen. Ah, warm!

I remind Pop that Mr. Appleby said to look forward. "If you can't look forward, at least look up," I say to Pop. "See the stained-glass window with the Miss Mitzi colors."

I want to be sure Pop remembers you.

I love you, Miss Mitzi.
Rachel

P.S. I leave food for Clarence every day so he won't starve. I hope he's the one who is eating his dinner and not some other animal.

P.S. again. This place is really not so terrible. There's plenty of wood, and even in this cold, Pop has dragged the old rugs outside and beaten the dust out of them the way we did with the mattresses. It's warmer now that there aren't so many holes in the roof. Pop and Joey have done a great job with that. Sometimes we knock icicles off the porch and crunch on them.

And again! I have to say the washing situation is not good. We have to bring pails from the stream to wash. Cold! And the laundry isn't working very well, either. We wash our clothes in cold water and hang them on a line outside. They dry stiff as boards!

SPRING

Dear Miss Mitzi,

Pop finally got a job at a grocery store. The man can't pay him much, but instead he is giving us food, mostly turnips, potatoes, and jars and jars of green beans. Cassie held one of the jars up to the light. "Slimy," she said. "You'd have to be starving."

Pop says President Roosevelt has great plans for his first hundred days in office. It's called the New Deal. Roads and forests are going to be fixed up; a huge dam will be built in Tennessee. This will put people back to work. Pop has his fingers crossed.

It's strange living here without neighbors. Back home, someone is always walking along the street or riding the trolley. Here, everyone is far apart. We just have each other, but sometimes a little of Cassie goes a long way.

Everyone loves your letters. Pop runs his hands over the edges as he reads. He misses you, I know it. I miss you, too. You are the best. And one more thing, thank you for all the stamps. I had only one left.

Love,
Rachel

CHAPTER TEN

Pop carries a bag and a crate in the door. He's home early from the store, because Mr. Brancato, the owner, closed at four. "No one is buying groceries," Pop says. "Everyone is making do with what he has."

"Food!" Joey pounces on the bag. He and Cassie open it to see what Mr. Brancato has sent home today.

Cassie sighs. "Potatoes again."

I look over their shoulders. The potatoes have spots and dents. By the time we cut out the bad parts, they'll be enough for only one meal. Never mind. Pop is great at adding stuff to them: a few onion slices, a little melted cheese. My mouth waters.

But I'm looking at the crate. What might it hold? Oranges and bananas? Cake with frosting? Strawberry ice cream? Ridiculous. "What is it?" I ask Pop.

"Eggs."

"Eggs!" the three of us say together. It's a bitter disappointment; I feel like the girl of the Limberlost in that book I read last winter.

Cassie looks as if she could burst into tears.

"Don't be so . . . orange," I tell her, trying to act as if I don't care.

"You're always talking like an idiot," she says.

Pop puts the crate on the table. "Not ordinary eggs," he says.

"Golden eggs," I say, "laid in the land of King Midas."

"I told you," Cassie tells the ceiling. "She's lost her mind."

Pop throws up his hands. "Will you two stop so I can tell you—"

Joey is taking the top off the crate carefully. "I bet I know," he says. "Eggs that will become chickens."

"Exactly," Pop says.

We crowd around him now and look at the twelve eggs nestled in straw pockets. Pop smiles at us as he moves the crate close to the fireplace. "We'll have to keep them warm and turn them five times every day. They'll crack open in three weeks."

He runs his hands over them. "Later they'll all go into the barn."

I reach out to touch one of the smooth white tops. Inside are the beginnings of tiny chicks.

Pop looks really happy; I feel happy.

He begins to cut the potatoes. "Water?"

We're supposed to take turns. We look at each other.

It's the worst job on the farm. Cold and wet, lugging the full pots back from the stream . . .

Whose turn is it?

"Not mine," Joey says. He's right; he's done it all week to give Cassie and me a break.

Cassie and I point at each other. She narrows her eyes. "I remember doing it last."

"So do I."

"You're always trying to get away with things, Rachel. You don't do the dishes, you don't sweep up. You're lazy."

I feel a little guilty, but I won't let her know she's right. "You're a pain in the neck."

"Girls," Pop says.

I pull on my coat and grab the pots by the handles. "Just remember, Cassie," I say over my shoulder, "you owe me."

"I owe you nothing," she says.

I slam the door behind me. Outside, there's still some light. It's not getting dark as early as it did even a week ago. Birds fly overhead in a V formation.

I walk along the fence, breathing in air that smells like spring and remembering the snowy night with that mean boy. Where is he now? Halfway to the stream, I hear the door open behind me. It's Pop.

"Cassie said she'll finish the potatoes," he says. "I'll walk with you."

He takes one of the pots and I put my free hand in his large pocket. Miss Mitzi comes into my head. "I think of her a lot." I touch the locket around my neck.

He knows who I'm talking about. "I do, too," he says without asking.

"I know she'd come in a minute."

We reach the stream. Fringes of green are beginning to show themselves along the muddy edges. I wait for Pop to answer as we dip the pots into the shallow freezing water so they'll fill.

"Pop?"

"We'll catch trout here soon," he says.

"We'll have hens," I remind him. "And I have enough money from my birthday for a goat. It's the beginning of a real farm."

"You're a nice girl," he says out of the blue.

Smiling, pleased to be a nice girl even though I'm a little lazy, I pull up the pot, the icy water sloshing onto my hands.

"Someday . . ." His voice trails off. Is he thinking about Miss Mitzi? He begins again. "We'll need more than eggs and hens and a goat."

"We'll have a garden, right? We'll grow our own potatoes. We'll have vegetables . . . carrots and pole beans." I try to think of something else. "Steak," I say, and we both laugh.

"I wish I could work at a bank. It's work I know." He spreads his hands. "But I have to do something, anything, so that money comes in. This grocery store job is a joke. I worked all day for a bag of potatoes and a dozen laying eggs."

We start back to the house. It's almost dark now. Cassie has lighted the gas lamp in the kitchen and there's a glow from the window. We can't see the peeling paint from here, and the house is much bigger than our old apartment. I'm surprised at the sudden warmth I feel. "Miss Mitzi would say it's inviting. If President Roosevelt gets rid of this depression, maybe we could ask her . . ."

Pop turns to me. "Oh, Rachel."

But I have a hopeful feeling. From now on, I'm going to do everything right. I'm going to get the garden ready as soon as I can. We'll get that goat one of these days. We'll get the barn ready.

Oh, President Roosevelt, please hurry.

CHAPTER ELEVEN

It's a Tuesday morning in April. Outside, it's beautiful; but it's still cold in here. I rub my feet together in bed and angle my head to glance at the drawings that march around the wall.

I feel as if I know the artist, that corkscrew tail she's given the dog, the duck with its beak high in the air. I can almost hear it quacking. The girl must have been smiling, maybe laughing, as she drew them.

Last night I finished my Rebecca book in one burst. I just couldn't make myself stop turning the pages; it was wonderfully cozy reading by the gas lamp in the kitchen with my coat tucked around me.

Cassie is standing in the doorway. "Are you ever getting up?"

"This minute." I throw back the covers and slide out of bed. The floor is gritty under my feet, but that's all right.

I'll sweep the whole thing as soon as I can get to it. I have more important things to concentrate on. I'm determined now to get this farm going, the way President Roosevelt is determined to get the country going.

As I walk along the hall, the back window darkens and the wall suddenly loses its color.

"Joey!" I scream.

Head covering the window, he hangs upside down from the roof. "They'll hear you in Brooklyn," he calls.

I see now that Pop is holding on to him from above. It reminds me of Joey reaching for money in the sewer.

I stand there watching as boards begin to cover the last holes in the roof. I listen to the sounds of the hammer. The hall downstairs is darker now, except for the light coming through the stained-glass window. The sun spears a yellow edge and the wall is a kaleidoscope of buttery lights.

In the kitchen I turn the chicks' eggs, then cut a slice of bread. Yesterday Mr. Brancato gave Pop a jar of strawberry jam for payment. I spread some on the bread and a strawberry lands on the crust.

Fortuitous, Miss Mitzi would say.

I sit back taking delicate bites, then I crouch down and open the cabinet doors under the sink to see what is in there. In back is a large pot.

"What are you doing?" Cassie asks.

"Look at this. We can use this one pot for water at the stream instead of two. It might be easier."

"You need two for balance," she says.

I don't look at her. I pull out the pot, gingerly holding

the wire handle. The inside may be filled with cobwebs and even a live spider.

But there's no spider, alive or dead.

I sit back on my heels. The pot is filled with a small pile of drawings. The colored chalk has smeared a little, but the pictures are wonderful. There is one of the stained-glass window and a few of the field out back filled with cornstalks, their tassels waving in the wind.

There's one of the roof. Why would anyone want a picture of a roof, even one with no holes?

The last one shows the house with its shiny rooster on top. It's gray and lovely, without a shred of peeling paint in sight. A tray of seeds grows near the doorway.

Underneath the drawings is an envelope, a little dirty, and marked *marigold seeds*. I run my hands over the edges of the envelope. I can feel the bumps of seeds.

I grab my coat off the hook and put the envelope in my pocket. Outside, I look up at Pop and Joey crawling along the roof. My hands are clammy as I watch them.

I head toward the barn and spend an hour digging soil. I plant the seeds in a tray one by one. "Grow," I tell them.

I can't wait to tell Pop.

What a terrible surprise to go back into the kitchen and see him with his head in his hands. And is it possible that he's crying?

Crying, my pop.

How can that be?

CHAPTER TWELVE

I don't know what to do. I back into the hall before Pop sees me and tiptoe out the front door. I lean against the porch post and close my eyes. I raise my hands to run my fingers through my hair.

Pop must be thirty-seven? Forty? I don't even know. But I want to know this: what could make him cry?

Joey comes around the corner, lugging something. "Hey, kiddo."

He's carrying some kind of iron thing. He begins to whistle that song "Happy Days Are Here Again."

I put my hands over my ears. That's the last thing I want to hear.

He stops when he sees my face, but he pretends that everything's fine.

That's Joey. He's such a good egg.

He raises the iron thing in the air. "A pitcher pump. Pop and I found it in the barn."

I nod a little.

He leans forward. "We'll have water in the kitchen by this afternoon. You just move the handle up and down, and water comes out like magic."

I touch his rough jacket, with its missing buttons. "Pop's inside. And something's wrong." I stop short of saying he's crying. I can't tell on Pop that way.

Joey's foot digs into the mud. "He was quiet before, really quiet. All he said was that we had to fix the roof right away and get the water in. He seemed to be in such a hurry."

We walk around to the back and Joey peers in the kitchen window. He draws in his breath.

For a moment we're quiet. Then Joey taps my arm. "You have to be the one to go in there, Rachel. You're the best of us, the smartest."

I'm horrified. Just horrified. "I can't, but thank you, anyway."

"What we can't do is let him sit there by himself," Joey says.

I swipe at the tears on my cheeks. What's that word? *Fortitude.*

"You're right." I smooth down my hair, which is in corkscrews all over the place, and head for the door.

I slide into the chair across from Pop and look down at a brown paper bag. He's scribbled numbers all over it. We sit there, not saying anything. Pop straightens the papers in front of him.

"What?" I ask after a while; my voice is so low I can hardly hear it myself.

Pop shakes his head. "We can't—"

It must be the farm. Something's wrong with it; everything's wrong with it. But we can't go back to the city; I know that. The city is forever away. And I realize I'm not ready to give up on this farm, bad as it is. There are the drawings; and the seeds, which won't live without a few sips of water every day; and the eggs, of course.

And what about Clarence? I still bring food to the fence every day.

"Money," Pop says. His voice is as low as mine.

"But the New Deal. President Roosevelt—"

"It will take time," Pop says.

If only I could make him feel better. Should I remind him of the stained-glass window, of the chicks that will hatch someday soon, or of the frilly plants growing at the edge of the stream that Miss Mitzi would love?

Pop runs his hand over the brown paper bag, over all those numbers. "I don't know what I was thinking. We'll never be able to get electricity. It'll be a dollar a month. And what about the rent? I just can't imagine."

"We don't need lights. We certainly don't—"

"We need coal."

"We don't need coal. We've got that fireplace. And sweaters." I try to smile. "It's getting warmer every day. And Joey says we'll have a water pump."

I see Joey then. He's sneaked around the front door and tiptoed through the hall. Cassie stands right behind him, her mouth opened in a little round O.

Pop looks toward the doorway. "I've lost my job at the grocery store," he says slowly. "It's not the man's fault. He has no money, either."

"Nothing to fear but fear itself," I try to say. Isn't that what the president said? But Cassie begins to cry. It's not the kind of crying I do. It's loud and it grates on my ears. Joey looks at me. It grates on his ears, too.

But Pop feels sorry for her. He holds out his arms, and she runs to him. "Here's the thing." He pats Cassie's back. "There's a job. It's a good job—"

"See?" Joey says. "I knew it would all work out."

But something's coming; I know it. Otherwise, what's all this about?

"President Roosevelt wants everyone to get back to work," Pop says. "And the town of North Lake will do what it can to help."

"Nice," Cassie says through her tears.

"They're going to build a road straight over the mountain near Canada. And they need workers."

I nod slowly. A job for Pop. But why would that make him cry?

Pop takes a breath. "A bus will take the workers up there." He looks at the three of us and shakes his head a little. "They won't come back for . . ." He hesitates. "A month. Maybe two months."

I sit back in my chair. The breath goes out of me. I know it's the only possible way we can get money. But still—being without Pop?

Cassie sees what's happening, too. Her cries are even louder.

But Joey jumps right in. "That's great, Pop. We'll manage. We'll get seeds going, the chicks hatched."

Cassie looks at Joey as if he's lost his mind.

Pop stares out the window. "How can I leave you alone? We have no neighbors nearby, and the town is far."

Joey cuts in. "Not alone. There are the three of us. Fine and dandy."

"I know you can take care of each other. . . ." Pop looks at each of us.

"I can't take care of Rachel," Cassie says. "And she can't take care of me."

"Cassie," Joey and I warn her.

Nothing to fear.

But I'm afraid. I'm certainly afraid. We'll have to stay here alone and, as Joey says, get things going.

I'm the oldest. I have to say something. "Don't worry, Pop. We can do this."

Joey and I glance at each other and then away.

Alone.

What a terrible word.

Dear Miss Mitzi,

I walked to town yesterday. It took all afternoon. I remember you said once that walking soothes the spirit.

My spirit needs soothing.

Pop is leaving next Monday for a job far away.

In town I watched the train come in with a huge whoosh of air. It was a cyclone of wind!

A woman with an old straw hat ran up to the train.

She handed the conductor a long cardboard box. It dripped all over him, but he smiled at her.

The woman smiled at me, too. "Ferns," she said, "to send to florists in the city."

I thought of you, Miss Mitzi, with your jars of ruffled ferns in the icebox. It seems forever since we've seen you.

Love,
Rachel

CHAPTER THIRTEEN

It's lonely without Pop. I wander into his bedroom, halfway down the hall. He's pulled the sheets up neatly over the mattress. Against one wall is a cabinet that he and Joey found in the cellar. On top is a picture of Miss Mitzi wearing her white straw hat. She's looking up, probably at Pop, who must have taken the photo last summer.

I straighten the doily beneath the picture and realize there's something under it. It's a letter and I know I shouldn't read it, but there are only a few sentences before it breaks off, and I see it all in one second.

Mitzi, my dear—
    Every day I think of asking you to come. If only I could do that. I miss you more than I can say, and the children

I touch the paper. Then, feeling guilty, I go to my room, closing Pop's door behind me. Later it takes me a long time to get to sleep. And then I feel myself dreaming. It's something about a new school. It's about a train and a box of ferns.

But then I'm awake. I tiptoe to the window. It's inky black outside, not a light anywhere.

I lean against the glass. I want Pop. I want him to be here. I want Miss Mitzi. Even though it's the middle of the night, I picture myself going to her flower shop. I'd sit in her back room, drinking sweet hot tea. It wouldn't be so dark. The city has lights at night, even small ones in the backs of the stores.

There's life outside here, Pop reminded us, even if there aren't neighbors. One night before he left, he talked about being on a farm when he was growing up. "We had a stream, too," he said. "I'd open my window at night and listen to the frogs croaking and the insects buzzing. Soon you'll hear that." He sat back, remembering. "There's so much going on under the water, fish gliding along, their mouths open, turtles taking slow steps."

I open the window, just a little, but I don't hear anything; it's quiet out there. I run my hand over the cold glass, comforting myself with thoughts of daddy longlegs climbing over the rocks, and birds fluffed up, asleep. I even picture chipmunks tucked under the rocks.

"Clarence, are you out there?" I whisper.

And where is Pop now? Before he left, we walked outside together and I know he was trying to cram everything into my head before he was gone. "I've paid the rent for

May," he said. "Be careful of money. You'll need it for June." He shook his head. "That's a long way off."

"Don't worry," I told him, my voice as strong as I could make it.

"It's a terrible thing to leave you on your own." I could hear the fear in his voice. "If we were in the city, there'd be people you could go to if you needed help quickly. But here, the closest neighbors are almost two miles away."

He put his hand on my shoulder. "There aren't any people near the farm, but Mr. Brancato at the grocery store would help." He hesitates. "The real estate man is there, too."

But I remembered what Pop had said to me once. *Chin out.* I said it back to him now. "We'll do this on our own. We don't need to ask for help." Then I added, "The three of us, you'll see."

When it was time for him to leave, we watched and waved from the mailbox as long as we could. In the early-morning light, he went down the road toward town with a small bag under his arm, hurrying to catch the bus. I thought about running after him but held on to the mailbox instead.

Now I look out the window at the dark. A gust of wind rattles the pane; it sounds like teeth chattering. I've left the bedroom door open, but I'm not sure that was such a good idea. The stairs creak as if someone is coming up them, and something scurries inside the walls.

Scurries?

A mouse?

I tiptoe to close the door. "Only Mickey Mouse," I whisper, shivering. "Only Minnie Mouse."

It takes a long time for me to open the door again and poke my head out. Suppose something is in the hall.

What?

I can't imagine.

I look up at the stained-glass window, so different without the sunlight behind it. But then a pale shaft of light flickers beyond the glass. See, the moon is shining up there after all.

I hear a sound. Crying? Someone crying? I take a step back.

It's Cassie.

Only Cassie.

"What are you doing out in the hall?" I ask.

For a moment, I wish we were sharing a bedroom again.

"I'm hungry." She blinks hard. She doesn't want me to see her tears. "Starving. That was a terrible dinner."

I'd volunteered to cook pancakes, but when I tried to take them out of the pan, they crumpled up like miniature accordions. I'm certainly not hungry now. The accordions seem to have unfolded in my stomach. But I don't want to go back into my dark bedroom—not by myself.

I look at Cassie. She's afraid. She has always been afraid of the dark. "Let's go to the kitchen," she says, and we go down the stairs together.

There's still a glow from the fire and Cassie moves like a cheetah, climbing up on the counter, opening drawers. She finds a couple of cookies I made and tosses one to me, but I miss and it hits the table, sounding like a rock.

"Some cook you are," she says, but she's almost smiling.

"It was the first time I ever made anything. Miss Mitzi says it takes time to be perfect."

I don't have time to say another word. There's a shadow in the doorway. I let out a chilling scream.

Cassie screams, too. "*Aaaaa!*"

I reach for her, but Joey says, "What's the matter with you two?"

For a moment we just stare at him. Then Cassie's arm goes straight out, pointing at me. "Rachel's afraid of the dark. She's afraid of anything that moves." And then she raises one shoulder. "Me too," she says in a small voice.

Just those two words and I forget that we're always arguing. I want to put my arms around her.

"I have an idea," Joey says. "We could go back to sleeping in the living room."

And that's what we do. In the dark, we drag the mattresses out of the bedrooms and push them down the stairs. They bump along halfway and we have to give them another shove to get them to the bottom.

It's not easy, but we don't care. We're all glad to be sleeping here together.

I miss you, Pop.

Dear Miss Mitzi,

We are sleeping on the living room floor now. Early this morning I awoke, listening to sounds: Cassie breathing, and Joey snorting a little.

I could look out the window and see hundreds of stars.

Pop said there's life outside. And when it was almost light, I heard a red-winged blackbird chirping. He was saying: "Talk to me, talk to me."

In my head, I told him that without school, I won't have any important words. I told him how terrible it was not to go to the library for books. I said, too, that we can't even write to Pop yet. We don't know where he is.

That reminded me of the night last winter when we went up on your apartment roof. You showed us the Milky Way, which looked just like a path of milk across the sky. We saw the Big Dipper and the North Star. Pop told us that sailors in the olden days used that star to guide them, because it always pointed north. "It was almost like reading," he said.

"I'm glad we have books," you told him. "It's too cold to be outside reading stars."

We laughed as we went downstairs and had hot chocolate and sugar cookies.

Do you remember that night, Miss Mitzi? Sometimes when I remember happy things, it makes me sad.

Love,
Rachel

CHAPTER FOURTEEN

On Thursday a week later, I tiptoe into the kitchen before Joey and Cassie are awake. I want to check on the eggs. We've learned how to manage the fireplace so the fire never goes out. Inside the eggs, the growing chicks must feel toasty warm.

I bend over them and check the Xs we've marked on each one so we can tell which side is up. We've been careful to turn them five times every day. Maybe they get tired of lying on their backs or their stomachs.

"Come out," I tell them. "See the world. I have names for you: Abigail, Betsy, Constance—"

Joey rustles around in the living room. I close my mouth. This talking aloud to myself has got to stop. "Gladys," I whisper, my nose an inch above the eggs.

But right now I have other things in mind. I pull on my coat, wind my woolly scarf around my neck, and cut a slice of bread. I bite off chunks that are rock hard. They take a long time to soften in my mouth.

Out front, I flip open the mailbox even though I know it's still too early for mail. A tan spider has moved in; he's spinning a poor-looking web that waves out to nowhere. Maybe even spiders are feeling the Depression.

I start down the road, swiveling my head back and forth; on one side are the trees, still bare; on the other side is our field. Pop has money in a mayonnaise jar for seed so he can plant corn when he comes back.

I'm enjoying the view, but I look for Clarence, of course, and I keep my eyes open for mountain lions.

Nothing to fear.

There's something I want to see up close. It's a really long walk, but I want to see this place alone, in all its faded glory.

I love that. *Faded glory.*

And there it is, up ahead.

The Warren Harding School.

"Hello," I whisper. It's just like a picture of a school I saw once in a book. It has a bell on top and it hasn't been painted in a thousand years.

I walk across the grass, which is mostly mud, and peer in the window, but all I see is a vestibule with a bunch of hooks.

Sad little hooks with no coats, no hats.

I wander around the back. Just over my head the window is open the tiniest bit. I stand there, chewing on the edge of my nail. Should I?

And even as I ask myself, I know I'm going to do it. I look around for something to boost myself up. And like magic, I see the milk crate against the wall.

Standing on the wooden crate isn't enough. I have to reach way up to grab the sill, and there's no way to push open the window.

I retreat to figure out how to get in. I see that I've left a muddy smear on the wall.

A row of rocks marches along at the edge of the trees. I spend ten minutes bringing the larger ones back to the milk crate. It looks as if I'm building a mountain. It feels that way, too. I'm a little out of breath.

I stand back and look at my work. Excellent.

I step up on the rocks and now I can use one hand to shove up the window. I wiggle like a worm and throw myself over the sill and inside.

Hands on my hips, I take a few breaths and look around. I'm in a little hallway, and there's a classroom on each side. Only two? I close my eyes. My school in the city has three floors of classrooms, all the way from kindergarten to eighth grade.

Look forward, Rachel.

One classroom must be for the little kids. Wiggly drawings of rabbits are tacked up on the wall: one has ears as long as the paper.

Across the way is the room I might be in. There's a painting of a tree, and underneath are the words *a nest of robins in her hair.*

I say that aloud; the sound almost echoes.

I would have loved being in this room. I see something else, drawings of daffodils . . . not bad, better than I could do. I stand in front of the room, taking the pointer from the ledge. "Today we are going to learn about my city," I tell a nonexistent class. "There's a ferry that goes back and forth across the river, and a bridge. Dozens of stores are open along the streets."

Wait a minute.

Bunnies down the hall, spring flowers here. I lean against the wall, tapping my lip. The desks have a film of dust over them. The windows are filthy.

The pictures aren't from this spring, but maybe last spring. What happened to fall leaves and Thanksgiving? What happened to drawings of sleds and snowflakes?

Has the school been closed for a year? I gulp down my disappointment. If it's been closed this long, who knows when it will open again?

Halfway down the hall, I peer into what must be the principal's office. The window is shattered; shards of glass lay on the sill, and a vase is on the floor with faded flowers and leaves scattered around.

I remember Miss Mitzi spilling the irises the afternoon I told her we were leaving. And then another memory of those happy days: all of us shopping and Pop buying Miss Mitzi a flower, which she pinned on her collar. Imagine. Buying a flower for someone who has a flower shop. But Miss Mitzi loved it. I could tell by the color of her cheeks.

Now I step inside and around a chair that's been

turned over to look at the desk; it has nothing on it, not even a blotter.

But behind the desk are books on a shelf: *The Wizard of Oz*, *A Girl of the Limberlost*. I bend down and run my fingers over a book called *Understood Betsy*. There must be a dozen books here, not being read, just alone on those shelves, waiting. . . .

Waiting?

Suppose I borrowed one.

Could I do that?

It wouldn't be stealing if I brought it back. Wouldn't it be just borrowing?

Outside, a cloud covers the sun; the light in the room is gray now. I shiver. I hear a noise.

Is someone walking down the hall? I stand there, frozen, but maybe it's just the wind. I peer into the hallway. No one. But still, I heard something.

I take two books off the shelf. I don't even see which ones they are. I fly down the hall and fumble with the door, but I can't get it open. I go back to the window and scramble out backward, scraping my wrist as I reach for the stones on the milk crate.

There they are. I'm free.

I dust myself off, and then I see something moving between the trees out back. Is it a deer? But the movement stops.

Is someone watching me? Is it the boy from the first night? The mountain lion boy?

Too bad there isn't snow. I'd—

But maybe it isn't the boy. Maybe it's the teacher.

Quickly I edge around the front of the school, and then I head for home. I have a terrible feeling in my chest. Whatever made me sneak in there? But then I know. I was hoping I'd see something, find something, to remind me of what school is all about.

The books under my coat feel heavy. One edge digs into my skin.

What have I done?

Dear Miss Mitzi,

Yesterday we kept watching the eggs. They were twenty-one days old. "Hurry," I kept saying.

Cassie said, "A watched pot never boils."

But Joey said, "I'm glad these are eggs and not pots."

At last the eggs began to crack open. Pop had warned us not to help them. "They have to fight their way out by themselves," he said. "Otherwise they won't be healthy."

We held our hands behind our backs so we wouldn't reach out and pull off a piece of shell here and there. They had to struggle so hard to get out.

But then out they came.

At first the new chicks were bedraggled, but they dried into yellow fluff. And someday they'll lay eggs of their own.

I wish you could see them.

Do you remember last year? We went to a duck

farm. All of us. You made a picnic lunch. We sang
"Old MacDonald Had a Farm."

Love,
Rachel

P.S. Did you ever do anything and didn't think
about it until afterward? Then deep down you knew it
was wrong?

CHAPTER FIFTEEN

I'm awake early every day, snuggled in bed, reading.

I'll hate to finish *Anne of Green Gables*. I wish I were just like her. I'd love that good, quiet Matthew, too. But sometimes I stop reading, keep my place in the book with my finger, and wonder: what would Anne say to a girl who'd sneaked into school and borrowed books without asking?

This morning, for the first time, I hear the frogs croaking down at the stream. I tiptoe into the kitchen and open the door to hear them better.

Yes, there they are, just as Pop said. If only he were here to listen to them with me. If only!

I sit at the kitchen table with the money he left us, listening to the chicks peeping in their box. I arrange the dollar bills with their gold seals in front of me, placing them separately, one by one.

A few days ago, with the money from the mayonnaise jar, the dollars covered almost the whole table. Now there's a hole in the middle. Where did it all go? Before he left, Pop brought home as much food as he could, but we took that long winding road to town and bought seed for the chicks from the grain store.

What else?

Milk from a farmer on the other side of town.

But what is here has to last us until we hear from Pop. No wonder I couldn't have a dog, or even a goldfish.

I remember Pop saying, "I'll send money as soon as I can." He ran his hand through his hair until it poked up in all directions, a sure sign of how worried he was. "I don't know how long it will take before I'm paid, or before I'll be able to send mail. I don't even know how much money it will be."

Cassie clatters into the kitchen, yawning, her hair a whoosh around her head. "It's not a good idea to have our money floating around all over the place." She pushes her bangs off her forehead.

I think of Pop reminding us at the last moment, "You'll have to learn to live together, to help each other."

Gaa, I wanted to say, but then I had a quick thought of Cassie climbing the tree in Brooklyn, holding out the pillowcase for my poor Clarence.

"Want some breakfast, Cass?" I say. "There's some cereal."

Cassie shakes her head. Her hair flies. "I'll do it myself, thank you."

It doesn't sound like a real thank-you. What's the matter with her this morning? And then I realize it's Pop's being gone. "I know, Cassie. I feel sad, too."

"I wish he'd write to me," she says. "I'd write back in two minutes."

Joey comes into the kitchen, his eyes still half closed.

Cassie cuts an uneven slice of bread and takes a huge bite. "Let's divide the money into three equal parts."

I frown at her. "What are you talking about?"

"That way it will be even-steven. Some for you, some for Joey. Maybe he'd like a new rooster for the roof." She looks like the cat that got the cream. "And some for me, of course."

I stare at her, then sweep the dollar bills off the table onto my lap. Forget about tree climbing and pillowcases and saving a poor cat. But then I remember Pop putting his hand over mine. "The only way this will work," he said, "is if you and Cassie are friends."

I try to stay calm. "The money's not for me. It's for the rent, for food. We'll need to be careful." My voice sounds like Pop's. I spread out my hands and a dollar floats onto the floor.

"I want to paint my bedroom," Cassie tells us. "Solid gold. It'll be gorgeous."

I bend over to pick up the dollar and another one flies off my lap.

"I'm just going to take a little—" Cassie dives for it.

We scramble on the floor. Her fingers, with the bitten nails, are quicker than mine. She picks up the dollar and grabs another one off the floor. "Just a can of paint," she says in the freshest voice I could imagine.

"It's only a can of paint." Joey echoes her. His voice is soft. "Come on, Rachel."

"I'll bring back the change . . . tons of change, you'll see," she says.

I see Pop going down the list of expenses. He tried to smile. "There's a song 'Brother, Can You Spare a Dime?' But you won't even have a nickel to spare."

"All right," I tell Cassie. How am I going to say what comes next? "We do have to divide—"

"Yes, three ways," Cassie says.

"The work," I say.

Cassie blows air through her teeth. "What work?"

"There's cooking and the chicks to feed and a garden to begin . . ."

Cassie's nodding. Nodding? "We have to keep this place clean." She glares at me. "You probably have jelly all over the money."

It's true she's much neater than I am. She likes everything dusted, organized, in its place. For the first time, I wonder what it's like for her to live in this mess of a farm.

But I keep talking over her voice. "Listen!" I smile, because I have coins in my pocket, my birthday money. "I have money for a goat. It's just a start. We won't have milk for a long time."

Joey jumps up. "That's great," he says through a mouthful of cereal.

Cassie cuts another slice of bread for herself. "Now we're getting somewhere. A gold bedroom and a goat."

"We have to get the weeds out of the garden, too," I say, "so we can plant."

"Gaaa," Cassie says, looking out the window.

"It will give us food. Vegetables . . ." I try to remember which ones she likes. What will make her go out there with me?

"How about Brussels sprouts?" Joey says.

She looks horrified.

"Tomatoes," I say. "Fresh tomatoes. " It's almost as if I were talking to myself. She loves tomatoes. For some reason, she puts sugar on them.

She does that Jell-O thing with her cheeks. "I could probably cook better than you do," she says. "If you plant the tomatoes, I'll make bread crumbs for them and you'd have to cook"—she looks up at the ceiling—"only once a week."

I'm not going to win this. I try to bargain. "You could clean the kitchen, too."

She looks around, but before she answers, I tell Joey, "Come on. Let's go out there."

He nods and follows me out the kitchen door.

Dear Pop,

I decided I'm going to write you a letter, even though I can't send it until we have your address. Cassie and Joey are writing, too. We are fine. How are you?

We have ten chicks in their box near the fireplace; two didn't hatch. When you pick the live ones up, they fit right in your palm. They are soft with scratchy little feet—no, I mean claws. Gladys is my favorite.

I am watching the money, just as you said. Cassie

intends to paint her room. She wheeled a wagon out of the barn and has gone to town. That way, she'll bring back the paint. It's a long walk. She'll be gone most of the day.

Don't worry. We're saving. Joey brought us something called fiddleheads from down at the stream. He said he read somewhere that you can eat them, so Cassie boiled them up. They are green with a taste that makes your hair want to stand up straight.

We ate them anyway, to keep up our strength. This means we didn't spend the money for two suppers.

Please write to us as soon as you can. We look for mail every day. Joey and Cassie send their love. I do, too.

Rachel

CHAPTER SIXTEEN

Upstairs is different in the daylight, bright and cheery. Why is it always so unfriendly in the dark?

I get dressed, talking to the duck on the wall. Then I run my fingers over each of my old treasures. "I'll never forget the city," I whisper so even the duck doesn't hear me. I picture Charlie the Butcher and Mrs. Lazarus. I remember Mr. Appleby, look forward. Of course, Miss Mitzi.

And, oh, Clarence.

I look toward the stack of letters on the windowsill, all from Miss Mitzi. Cassie and Joey have piles of letters from her, too.

I go through the letters looking for the one about cats and read part of it. It's as soothing as a cup of sweet hot tea.

My cat Lazy did come back. I have my fingers crossed that Clarence will, too. Maybe he has to get used to

North Lake. Maybe he's exploring. One day he might say to himself, "Hey, I'd better find out how my old friend Rachel is." You'll look out the window, and there he'll be, waiting for a handout, just like a hobo. I wonder how my old friend Rachel is, too. Missing all of you is like a toothache. I take out a memory every day and it makes me happy again.

The letter sounds exactly the way Miss Mitzi talks. I wipe my eyes and look out at the garden. It's still full of long reedy grass and stones, which Joey and I keep pulling and tossing.

Yesterday I felt blisters coming up along my palm, and Joey dropped a rock on his foot. After a while we felt a few drops of rain. "Put your head up, Rachel," Joey said. "Taste the water on your tongue."

We felt like pioneers in the desert.

But then it poured. Rivers of rain ran along the soil, making little furrows. In two minutes we were full of mud, so we rushed inside.

It seemed forever before Cassie came back, trudging down the road, her wet hair plastered to her head. She came slowly, pulling the wagon with the can of paint through the ruts in the road.

I opened the door for her and I could see she was ready to cry. I didn't have the heart to ask her about the change from the paint. Maybe tomorrow.

From upstairs, I can hear her working the pump in the kitchen. I hear the up and down creaking, then water splashing into the sink. I love that sound. And who would have believed I'd love poking my head and my hands under that gush of icy water to wash my hair and my clothes? It's so much easier than bringing water from the stream. I almost miss going down there with the pots, though. I always stopped to watch the water bubbling over the shiny rocks and see the small arrows of green poking up their heads between the wide leaves of the skunk cabbages.

In the kitchen we cut the last of the bread and spread it with jam. It's a good thing there's a box of crackers up on the shelf left over from the apartment.

Then we set off. We're on the way to bring home a goat. Someday we'll have milk!

Goat's milk, which I've never tasted, but still . . .

Joey is way ahead of us, because Cassie and I are bouncing a ball, playing that game. It's my turn: "W my name is Wilma and my husband's name is Woodrow—"

"The cat's name," Cassie says.

"What are you talking about? Woodrow Wilson was a president."

"It's the cat's name," she says firmly.

I miss and the ball bounces away from me. It's impossible to have a friendship with Cassie. Now she's naming my cat.

"Clarence," I say, and catch my breath, because Joey's reached a bridge over the river.

Before I can stop him, he climbs up and begins to walk along the outside of the railing. He teeters, then balances himself, one arm out; one foot edges in front of the other.

My hand goes to my mouth. I want to yell at him to get down, but I'm afraid if I do, he'll fall. Next to me, Cassie is frozen.

A moment later, Joey sails off at the end. Safe!

I let out my breath. Joey, always doing something dangerous.

I do yell now. "What's the matter with you? Have you lost your mind?"

But he just grins at me.

A few steps, and Cassie and I stand at the bridge to look down: a terrifying drop. "Don't ever do that again," I call after him, but I could be talking to the air. Already he's way ahead of us again.

We pass the school, with its faded drawings on the windows. My throat tightens. I just have to hope that no one saw me that day. I've spent every free minute reading *Anne of Green Gables*, but with every page, I know I shouldn't have taken those books.

Cassie gives the ball a bounce. "X my name is—" she begins, and breaks off. "It's the best luck in the world that the school is closed."

I know she's buying time so she can think of a name that begins with X, but still it reminds me that there isn't one thing we agree on.

Ahead of us, Joey stops at the gate with the sign: GET YOUR GOAT.

We walk up the path and angle back toward the barn. The goat lady sits on the ground, her legs stretched out in front of her. Next to her is a gray goat with pale green eyes and two small horns next to her ears.

The goat lady looks up and smiles. "We've been waiting for a buyer," she says. "Xenia and I."

"Is that with an X?" Cassie asks.

The goat lady nods. "She's my twenty-fourth goat. I'm going right through the alphabet. Maybe because I'm a teacher." She smiles at us. "Mrs. Collins."

Cassie and I look at each other. X my name is Xenia. Then I stare at Mrs. Collins. "A teacher?"

She's still patting Xenia. "The school is closed." She leans forward. "Do you know that schools have been closed in twenty-four states?"

"Because of the Depression?" I say.

"Exactly."

I shake my head, but Cassie puts her arms around the goat's neck. She looks thrilled for the kids in twenty-four states, especially herself.

"In the meantime," Mrs. Collins says, "someone broke into my school. . . ." She looks as if she's going to cry.

I feel heat creeping up my neck.

She tries to smile. "But you're new." She closes her eyes. "Let me guess. You live on the farm with the stained-glass window."

"Yes." I hope she doesn't see that my face is red. I want to blurt out, *I wasn't the one, I would never—*

"You walked a long way," she says. She begins to tell us how to take care of the goat. What to feed her. How to keep her warm and happy. That goats like to eat strange things.

I can hardly listen. If only I could tell her I'd give anything to go back to school, to learn new words, to write . . . write letters, write poetry, write anything.

She must see that I want to say something. She stops talking, one hand in the air. Her eyes have lines around them. She squints and the lines become deeper, almost like rays of the sun.

"It's just . . ." I shake my head.

She smiles, waiting.

But I never say any of it, because I see a flash of something from the corner of my eye.

I turn quickly. Is that the mountain lion boy, standing behind a fence, back by the trees? I can almost hear his voice. *You don't belong here.* I take a step back.

Mrs. Collins doesn't see that. She waits for a minute more, but then she gives us a bag of feed. "To start you off."

"Thank you," Joey and Cassie say together, but I'm still staring over Mrs. Collins's shoulder.

She turns. "The stream out back is great for trout."

She waves at the boy. He has a fishing pole in his hand, Was he at the school that morning? Was he the one who saw me?

"Would you like to see the cows?" Mrs. Collins asks, but before Cassie or Joey can answer, I say, "We have to get home. We have to get the goat settled."

For once Cassie doesn't argue. I can't imagine why, unless she sees how anxious I am to get out of there.

I take Xenia by the rope Mrs. Collins has tied around her neck and lead her down the driveway, listening to the bells on her collar.

When we reach the road, I stop and look back over my shoulder.

"What's the matter with you?" Cassie says.

I turn to Joey. "Did you see that boy fishing?"

He shakes his head.

I breathe again. We take turns leading the goat, petting her, and I'm so glad to glimpse the house ahead of us that I smile at Cassie.

Dear Miss Mitzi,

Our goat is thriving. Xenia was supposed to live in the barn, but Cassie thought she'd be lonesome with only the marigolds to keep her company.

So now we have hay in the pantry for Xenia's bed. She loves to eat apples and raisins and my socks.

She's a climber. She stands at the window with her front hooves on the low sill, chewing her cud. . . . Is that what they chew?

I miss learning words with you, Miss Mitzi. I love the sounds of them, the feeling of letters on my tongue and in my throat. I have to tell you that I talk to myself. Sometimes I make up words to go with whatever I'm thinking.

We miss Pop so much. Our letters are piling up on the table, waiting to be sent, and still we don't hear from him. It's a worry . . . such a worry.

And wanting to go to school is like wishing for Christmas. But I've done something I shouldn't have. Every time I think about it, I go outside and run across the field to stop remembering what I've done. Sometimes it works. Sometimes it doesn't.

Love,
Rachel

CHAPTER SEVENTEEN

This morning, I stand in my bedroom with Miss Mitzi's letter in my hand and read a piece of it aloud: "'Look in the mirror and tell yourself what you did wrong, Rachel. Then figure out how to fix it no matter how hard that is. Know that I love you.'"

I stare at the mirror, with its wavy lines. "I shouldn't have broken into the school. I shouldn't have borrowed those books," I say aloud.

I know I have to go back to the school. At least I've finished *Anne of Green Gables*. I loved it when she said her life was a graveyard of buried hopes. I close my eyes and wish there were a house down the road and Anne lived in it.

I sit on the floor and read a couple of pages of *Understood Betsy*, but I'll never get to finish it now. Then I tiptoe downstairs with the books, careful not to wake Joey and Cassie, and let myself out. It's early; a few stars are visible and a dusty moon lights the road ahead.

By the time I reach the school, daylight has edged its way up over the trees, and the moon has become a pale white sliver.

I wait for a few minutes, making myself count to one hundred and then another hundred, but no one's there. "Poor school," I whisper. "All alone with nobody getting ready to come for the day. No teachers. No children."

At last I walk around to the back, on tiptoes again even though there's no one to hear. The box is still there under the window, but a few weeds have begun to sprout around it.

It takes only a few minutes to climb inside and go down the hall to the principal's office. I slip the two books back onto the shelf, filling the space where they belonged. I touch all the books; I have nothing new to read now and no way of getting a book. I run down the hall and climb out the window. I toss the stones and the box away, and I'm on the road.

Safe.

But not safe. I see a boy and I know who he is. And he sees me, too.

I take the long walk home and let myself into the kitchen. Cassie sits at the table, holding her head in her hands. I remember Pop sitting at that same spot, the day he told us he had to leave.

If only we could hear from him.

"What's wrong?" I ask Cassie.

She doesn't answer. She gets up and works the pump at the sink, up and down, up and down; the water splashes.

What can I say? "I wish I had something new to read," I tell her at last.

"Is that all you think about?" she asks. "Always with your nose in a book instead of doing something instructive."

"Constructive."

"What a know-it-all you've turned out to be," she says. "Just read that Betsy book."

I can't tell her it's gone.

But she's on to something else. "When does the man come for the rent?"

"Soon."

She leans her head against the pump, but before I can figure out what's the matter, Joey comes into the kitchen. "Ready to work on the garden?" he asks.

Cassie turns. "How about going fishing?"

We both blink. Cassie hates fish.

But Joey and I love fish. Pop used to cook smelts at home, and sometimes fluke.

"We need to save," she reminds us.

I can't believe it. She's worried about money.

Joey looks at me.

"Sure," I say. "I'll work on the garden."

Before I go outside, I lean over the gate we've put up. Xenia's eating some of the food Mrs. Collins gave us. She wiggles her nose with each bite and I pat her long ears.

In the barn I find a cloche hat on a hook. The felt is torn and dusty but I pull it down over my hair like a bell.

It reminds me of Miss Mitzi in the blue cloche that matches her eyes, her curls escaping from the sides. Miss Mitzi, ready to take me shopping at the department store on Fulton Street.

Ah, Miss Mitzi.

I look around. I'd like to lie there in the hay with a lovely new book—and forget about gardening. Instead, I drag out a bunch of farm tools, most of which are incomprehensible to me.

Is that the right word?

Is that even a word?

I think about my garden. I'm going to make it even bigger than the one Joey and I began. I bend over, using a shovel. I hack away, but almost nothing happens. The ground is hard as cement.

Overhead, the sun is strong. It's much too hot for the hat. I toss it over my shoulder and hack some more. And then I start to get into the rhythm of it. Dig, dig deeper, turn the weeds up, the soil up.

After a while, I throw myself on the warm earth. I grab a long brown weed and yank it. And then another.

Lying there, I keep pulling. I can see the clear spot becoming larger, the edge of the garden uneven, but satisfying. I get on my knees and reach for a trowel that will fit in my hand. I rough up the ground . . .

And keep going.

At last Cassie raps on the kitchen window. It's lunchtime. I stand up and nearly fall over. My face is stiff; my knees ache; one foot is asleep.

I look down at my work. The earth is dark and rich.
I love the way it looks.

It's almost as good as reading.

In the kitchen, I'm surprised to see three plates with paper napkins underneath them. On each plate is a sandwich. The bread is cut unevenly, but I love the peanut butter and jelly.

"Best lunch I've had since Pop left," Joey says.

I gobble down the sandwich and then I go outside again. I wander into the barn to find a wheelbarrow that I saw the other day.

On the back wall is a drawing. It's rough, because the wall is rough. The picture shows a girl. She's reading a book that covers her face.

What is she reading?

Who is she?

Around the drawing is a pile of hay. From the way it's pressed down, I figure the artist must have knelt there as she drew.

I wheel the wheelbarrow outside and throw in the weeds I've pulled up. I spend the rest of the afternoon pulling and throwing, then emptying the wheelbarrow behind the barn.

From there I see the stream. Joey, his feet in the water, waves the fishing pole Miss Mitzi gave him. Beyond him, I see rows of fern.

Oh, Miss Mitzi, you'd love this.

I don't stop working until late in the afternoon, when Joey walks by with three fish on a string.

Poor things.

Never mind the poor things.

We need the food.

And it's free.

We eat the fish from head to tail. It's crispy; it's so good; I've never tasted anything so good. I thank Joey. I even thank Cassie.

She's a good cook; I have to give her that. And she's put a couple of wild onions and chives on top to cover the fish. "So we don't have to see their sad eyes," she says.

She looks sad, too. Her eyes are red. I wonder if she's been crying.

I try not to think about it. In the field, she's found wild strawberries for dessert. They're no bigger than my pinky nail, but they're sweet; we sit there, satisfied.

Imagine, strawberries!

But something's wrong with my face. I feel it and Cassie sees it. "Rachel's as red as a beet," she tells Joey.

"You're sunburned," he says.

"Didn't you wear a hat?" Cassie's eyes are narrowed, as if the sunburn is all my fault.

That Cassie.

My face is so stiff now, I can hardly open my mouth. I push my plate away and go into the living room to ease myself down on the mattress. The pain is worse every minute.

Joey comes in with thick white paste in a small bowl. "Baking powder and water," he says. "It's old and wormy, though. I found it in the cupboard."

I try to smile at him. I know he was remembering last

summer after a hot day swimming. Pop made the paste and spent the night slathering the three of us with it.

I don't care that Joey's paste is old, or even that it's wormy. I sit up and smear it over my face. It's cool and it helps. I dab some on the back of my neck, and so what that it's in my hair?

Then I sleep through until the next morning. I wake up as soon as it's light and roll off the mattress, easing myself up. As sunburned as I am, I can't wait to get outside to work on the garden. I can see the square of deep brown earth. I'll rake it until it's smooth and ready to plant.

The green plants will come up, and then we'll have vegetables!

Dear Miss Mitzi,

Today Cassie was crying in the kitchen. She says something must have happened to Pop, because he still hasn't written to us. I reminded her that he said it might be a while, even though I'm uneasy, too.

But Joey said maybe she's worried about something else. I asked him why he thought that, but he just raised his shoulders in the air.

I keep remembering her crying and how much I loved her when we were little. I don't know what happened to us. Cassie is mean; but I'm mean, too.

I tried to say something friendly. I began telling her about my Rebecca book.

After two minutes, she slammed down a plate. "If you cared so much about a book, you wouldn't be leaving it in the kitchen to get ruined."

"I do not. I certainly—"

She cut right in. "You like books better than me, anyway."

Joey put his finger to his lips, warning me not to say anything I'd be sorry about.

I tried something else. "How is your painting going?"

She burst into tears, went upstairs, and banged her bedroom door shut.

Maybe gold isn't such a hot color for an orange girl.

Love,
Rachel

Dear Pop,

I've been working on the garden. The earth is a wonderful chocolate brown. I used the rest of my birthday money to buy vegetable seeds and planted all of them. Afterward I made paper markers so I can tell what everything is—and where everything is. I even drew pictures with pink and purple pastels that were left on the secret stairs: wiggly drawings of radishes and carrots.

We're still sleeping in the living room. Xenia, the goat, is sleeping with us. We all love Xenia, especially Cassie. But Xenia loves chewing on the end of the mattress. She's made a hole in Joey's. The stuffing is coming out.

The chicks are in the kitchen. We have to be careful not to step on them. They skitter from one end to the other. They've lost their yellow Easter look and I have to say they're a little ugly, poor things.

Listen, Pop. Try to write when you can. I haven't spent any more of the money you left. It's in the kitchen cabinet. But I know we'll have to pay the rent, and we'll need food really soon. I'm a little worried, because that will be the last of the money.

Love,
Rachel

CHAPTER EIGHTEEN

It's usually hard to keep track of time, but one thing I'm sure of. I'll have to go to town on Tuesday and pay the rent. It will take almost every cent of what we have saved in the kitchen cabinet.

Two more days!

On my way downstairs, I pass Cassie's bedroom. She's up, painting; her room is almost finished.

In the living room, Xenia stands at the curtains—bile-green ones, Miss Mitzi would say. They were left by the old owners.

Xenia doesn't mind bile-green. She's eaten one curtain up as far as she can reach, and started on the next one.

"Hey," I say.

She turns, chewing thoughtfully, staring at me with those watery green eyes.

How can all that fabric be in her stomach?

I clap my hands at her. "You're going to the barn, lonely or not, as soon as I have time to make a place for you."

Outside, I breathe in the warm air and smile at my plants, pale strings that soon will be vegetables. I've planted the marigolds in the corners. Everything looks spectacular.

Over my head, birds fly back and forth. They swoop into the eaves of the house, working on mud nests as bumpy as warts.

If only I had something new to read! But that reminds me. My Rebecca book is up in my bedroom, not gathering stains in the kitchen as Cassie said. I'm going to wave it at her the next time we're upstairs, just to show her. And then I'm going to read it over again; I'll pretend I don't know what's going to happen.

I look up and see Cassie at the window. She looks so . . . woebegone. Strange word, but it fits. Her hair straggles over her collar, her cheeks are red, and she reaches up to wipe her eyes with the back of her sleeve.

I shake my head and go down to the stream. I sit there at the edge, untying my shoes; I pull them off and my socks, too. I leave them near a circle of feathery ferns and walk along the edge, the wet sand gritty against my feet. The stream turns, and there in the shade is a rock. More than a rock. A boulder.

A wonderful place to sit.

I bend over to dip my hands in the water. The blisters from gardening are healing into thick lumps and my palms are getting tough. I cup them, bringing them up to my mouth for a sip. Then I straighten, the hem of my dress soaked, and I see it.

On the rock is a drawing, big and bold. It reminds me of Mrs. Thompson, the art teacher. She came to our classroom once a week and drew all over the blackboard.

I never could tell what she was doing; she drew lines and circles, and she'd tell us to draw like that.

I tilt my head now, looking at these lines. But it's not the kind of art that Mrs. Thompson did. It's . . .

A girl, of course.

I bend for another sip of water, looking up at that girl. I can't see her face, because she's wearing a cloche hat with drops of rain cascading from the edges. Her dress is red gingham with a locket caught in the top buttons.

I stand entirely still.

Is she wearing my dress?

There's something covering her hands.

What is it?

In the warm sun, I wet my hair and soak my face and neck. I put on my hat as the water runs down my shoulders in rivulets, and keep staring at the drawing.

Does she look like me?

It is me! Something tugs in my mind. Something to do with the drawing in the barn.

That's me, too.

And—

I hear the sound of a motor. It's not the sound of the mail truck, though.

Amazing. Not once has a car come up the rutted path that leads to our house. I hear it stop.

I shade my eyes. Who could it be? Pop? Home from working on the road? I feel a quick flutter in my chest.

I start toward the house without my shoes and trip over a tree branch. For a moment I can't catch my breath. I scramble up, but by the time I reach the kitchen steps, there's the sound of the motor again, as the car drives away.

I burst in the door. Cassie stands in the hall, her back toward me. She's still, almost like a statue I saw at the museum one time.

"Who was it?" I look toward the living room, toward the window with its chewed curtains. The car has gone.

She doesn't answer.

"Cassie?"

Something is wrong, really wrong. I go toward her and spin her around. "Who?"

Joey comes down the stairs. "What's going on?"

"Nothing." Her voice is strange.

"Did I hear a car?" Joey asks.

She shrugs. "I don't know."

"But you were the one who was here, right here," I say.

She waves one hand and walks away from us and out the door.

Joey and I stand there looking after her, then we go into the kitchen.

"There was a car," he says. "I know it."

I know it, too. I want to go after Cassie, but from the open kitchen door, I see Xenia in my garden, a strand of green in her mouth.

CHAPTER NINETEEN

I scramble around the chicks and out the door; I run across the yard, yelling, waving my arms.

Xenia. Oh, Xenia.

She wiggles her nose at me, a bit of green edging its way into her mouth.

I pull her out of the garden, but it doesn't make any difference. The pale shoots are gone; the marigolds have disappeared. Nothing is left.

I sink to the bare earth as Xenia wanders off. All my work is ruined.

I begin to cry. I cry for my garden, for Clarence. I cry for Miss Mitzi and Mrs. Lazarus. I cry because there is no school and because I don't know where I'd get money for more seed. But most of all I cry for Pop. Where is he? Why hasn't he written?

It seems that every single thing I'm crying about has something to do with the Depression.

When I get up, I'm full of mud. Who knows where Xenia has gotten herself? I look around; she's back by the fence, her head up, enjoying the warm sun and her nice full stomach.

I walk along the fence and put my hand on her collar. She gives me a soft nudge. "Not your fault." I stroke her soft ears. "But it's the barn for you, ready or not."

I take her up to the barn, find a stall, shovel in some hay so she has a bed. I fill a pail with water from the stream, in case she needs a drink. All the while, I'm wondering about how to get seed. It's impossible.

Back in the house I sit in the kitchen. I sit there forever, it seems. Then Joey comes in. "Have you seen Cassie?"

It's past lunchtime, way past lunchtime. I shake my head.

"Listen, Rachel, maybe we'd better look for her. She's been crying."

"Missing Pop, missing the city?" I raise my shoulders. "We all feel that. But what about that car? Did that have something to do with it?"

Joey looks in the cabinet for something to eat. "Beans," he says.

I'm beginning to feel hungry, too. I stand next to him, peering into the cabinet: that row of jars filled with gray string beans, more jars of tomatoes, stale soda crackers. We munch on them. "It's not like Cassie to miss lunch," I say.

"She was crying," Joey says again.

"Maybe she's upstairs."

I go up to her room, open the door, and blink.

Gold. How can she live with that color? The paint can is set on an old piece of cloth, the brush washed and laid out neatly. It's just like Cassie to be so careful.

Downstairs again, I shake my head at Joey.

"She's still outside, then," he says.

I shove the cracker box back into the cabinet and see—

My hand goes to my mouth. Cassie's right. My Rebecca book is there on the counter. And yes, there's a spot of jelly on it. I turn the book over. It's not my Rebecca book. It's *Understood Betsy*.

But I brought it back to the school.

"I'll be out in a minute." I'm hardly able to talk. I run up to my bedroom. I look in the closet, on the windowsill, under the bed. *Rebecca* is gone.

I go downstairs slowly, trying to understand what happened. I see myself going around the back of the school, passing the flagpole, putting *Anne of Green Gables* and my Rebecca book on the shelf. I put my own book there!

On the inside cover of *Rebecca* is written *to Rachel, from S. Lazarus*.

The principal of the school will see it, too.

Joey stands outside the kitchen door, waiting for me. "I've looked down at the stream. She's not there. I've called and called."

"She went out the front door," I say, "not the back."

He nods.

"So she probably went to town."

He looks doubtful. "I hope she didn't go the other way."

"But there's nothing there. Just a dirt road."

"There's a cabin on the path up the mountain to the lake. Way up. I saw it once."

I shake my head. "She wouldn't go that way. Why would she?"

"Something's really wrong," Joey says.

Joey, who always believes everything is right, everything is fine.

My stomach lurches. "What are we going to do?"

CHAPTER TWENTY

We call until our voices are hoarse. And then at last we stop.

"Let's take the path past the cabin," Joey says.

"Wouldn't the road to town be easier?" I bend down. My shoelace is untied. The shoes are old; the sole on one foot has come unglued. It flaps a little. It will slow me down, but there's no help for it.

Joey stands there waiting. "Look at the sky," he says. "It will be dark soon. If she's gone to town, we don't have to worry about her. But the other way—"

I glance up to see a mass of clouds; they're rimmed with gold as the sun sinks behind the hills. I can feel the chill in the air. I wish I'd worn my coat instead of just this thin sweater. But Joey doesn't have to say anything else.

We turn off at the dirt road and walk for a long while. Ahead of us then is a small cabin. Off to one side is the beginning of a garden. In front, flowery curtains cover the windows.

We walk past; stones in the packed earth sound loud against my shoes. But inside the cottage, all is quiet, and the road turns before we see anyone.

It's narrower now and trees on each side cut off the light, almost like a Hansel and Gretel forest. I wonder, too, about animals. Could there really be mountain lions? Could there be a mother bear with cubs? What else? Snakes? Skunks?

Joey begins to whistle a little. I don't recognize the song; I can hardly hear it. I wonder if he feels the same strangeness that I do.

We keep walking, the road rising gently, but it's getting dark. I hear clicks and chirps and even a brrrr and move closer to Joey.

"Tree frogs," he says. "Maybe some insects."

Cassie is afraid of the dark, so afraid. Together we begin to call her. We cup our hands around our mouths to make our voices loud. The brrrr and the other noises stop; when we stop, they begin again. Every few minutes we call, Joey, then me, Joey, then me.

What made her do this? What happened? For a moment I remember the car that stopped in front of our house. An ordinary car, not the sound of the mail truck— I would have recognized that.

Isn't it odd that Cassie and I never get along? That we're so different? But so many times we've been friends: walking home from school together, getting caught in a rainstorm, running, laughing. Buying a bag of candy for

Joey's birthday and sneaking two pieces out for ourselves. Hanging stockings. Christmas morning. Dressing as beggars on Thanksgiving morning and knocking on doors for treats. I can hear Cassie's voice: "Anything for Thanksgiving?"

I wonder if Cassie remembers those things.

At the top of the hill, the road widens. In front of us is a shimmer of water. "North Lake," I say. "It must be." We stand at the rim, looking down at it scooped out of the hills. There aren't as many trees, so we can see for a long distance: a twinkle of lights miles away.

For the first time I begin to be afraid for Cassie. "She went to town," I say.

He stands looking down at what we can see of the lake, a circle of reeds at the far end, a mess of branches at the other. Could it be a beaver's den? Insects flit across the top, and something larger—a bat, I'm sure of it.

"Maybe she's home by now," Joey says.

"Of course, that's it." I feel such a relief, then I'm angry. It's cold and dark; it will be hard to see the road ahead of us. At least it will be downhill.

"Maybe we could stop at the cabin and ask if anyone's seen her," Joey says.

"It's getting late. Let's just go home. I'm sure . . ." The words trail off. I'm not sure, not at all sure, that she's home.

CHAPTER TWENTY-ONE

We run up the road to the house, looking for the gas lamp that will surely be lighted if she's there.

But it's dark.

We burst in the front door, down the hall, calling her. I run upstairs to her room, just in case. But of course she's not there.

In the kitchen I don't bother to fill the feed tray for the chicks. I don't have time for that. I just raise the heavy bag a couple of inches and dump it in a hill on the floor.

Oh, Cassie, where are you?

"Get your coat," I tell Joey, "and I'll get mine. We have to go out again."

But where?

"I'll go back to the cabin for help," Joey says. "Suppose she's in trouble somewhere?"

"You mean fallen?" I'm glad the stream is so shallow. But I picture her tripping over a rock. Breaking . . .

Bleeding?

He nods. Then he's gone and I wait.

I don't even care anymore that I think it's the mountain lion boy's cabin, as long as he'll help. Was he right that I don't belong here? That we don't belong here?

I look around. I didn't belong here that first day, or even the first month. But I love my garden, bare as it is. And what about the fireplace in the kitchen on cold nights, the drawings on the stairs, the stained-glass window? And there're Xenia and the chicks, who gather around my feet, pecking at their seed. I'm beginning to belong. I really am.

But suppose something happens to Cassie? That's worse than almost anything I can think of. Why didn't I know that?

I go outside and down along the fence to meet Joey and take a breath. The mountain lion boy is with him. I don't know what to say.

He hardly glances at me. "Hi," he says.

He looks as uncomfortable as I am. Ha. Serves him right. Then I remember: I'm the one who threw the snowball. I'm the one he saw in the school.

"Maybe the stream," he says, and Joey nods.

We walk along the edge of the water. A moon is up now; it beams along the water, almost leading us. Hansel and Gretel again!

I've lost the sole of my shoe, and mud seeps in, so I

take both shoes off and put them under a tree to find later. The stream leads us toward town. I see the back of Mrs. Collins's house, then, almost a mile after that, the real estate office, the grain store, the train station.

"Maybe she took a train," the boy says, his first words since we began to walk.

Back to the city? I shake my head. That would take money. She never gave me the change from the paint, though. Could she have used that?

There's no answer in my mind.

The stream peters out and the three of us walk back toward our house.

That's what I would have done. If I'd had trouble, I would have gone straight to Miss Mitzi.

But what trouble? What possible trouble?

We reach the back of our house; there are still no lights, no sign of Cassie. It must be almost midnight.

"What can we do?" I hold my hands out in front of me. "Maybe we have to get help."

"I'm sorry," the boy says. It looks as if he's talking to the ground.

"I'm sorry, too." Are we both talking about Cassie? I don't think so.

"Come inside." There's a little tea in the canister. Maybe . . .

He follows us and I light the gas lamp. "What's your name?" I ask at last.

"Anton."

I nod and then I remember Xenia.

She's been shut up in the barn for hours. True, she has hay and water, but no food. She must have digested the curtains hours ago.

"Just sit at the table," I say to them. "I'll be right back."

I grab up a scoop of goat food for Xenia and walk around the table. As I do, I glance at Anton. His hair is down over his ears; he's wearing a thin shirt. He must have been cold outside. His hands are covered with a smear of something blue.

I follow the fence around to the barn and slide open the doors. Xenia is in her stall. In the dim light I see that her eyes are closed; she's curled up against the wall, looking perfectly comfortable. "I'm sorry, Xenia," I say anyway. "I know you don't like to miss a meal."

Something else is in the stall with her. I see the outline of a figure and step back.

The dark shape moves and I'm ready to run. Then I see who it is. I sink to my knees. "Cassie." I'm crying now and I reach out to her and our hands meet over Xenia's back.

"What are you doing here?" I've never felt such relief. "I love you." I have to say that fast; already I want to yell at her for causing this whole mess. "Didn't you hear us calling? Didn't you know we'd be looking for you?"

"I didn't want to answer," she says. "I was going to run away, back to Miss Mitzi maybe."

I shake my head, wondering.

"But I didn't have any money."

"You had the change from the paint."

She's crying, too, now, a real Cassie crying, loud and grating.

Never mind. She's here and she's safe.

I crawl around Xenia. Cassie and I sit together, leaning against the wall of the stall. We hold hands. I can't believe that. We haven't been this close since we were little.

"I didn't have the change," she says at last. "I lost it somehow on the way home from the paint store. It was raining and I put my hands in my pockets. I don't know how the money slipped out. I went back and back, but it was gone."

I shake my head. Careful Cassie.

"The real estate man came this morning," she says.

"In the car? But he's early. The rent isn't due for two days."

Cassie shrugs. "I didn't have the money anyway."

"Of course we do. It's in the kitchen cabinet." I lean my head back against the wall. I'm so tired. It's hard to keep my eyes open. And both boys are waiting for me. I start to get up.

"No, it's gone. I lost that, too."

"What do you mean?" I sink back down.

"I took every bit of the money with me to town," she says, "to buy the paint."

Xenia makes a little sound of contentment. I shake my head. What is she talking about?

She says it again. "I took the money. I was angry. I was going to bring it back, but I don't know what happened to it."

The money's gone? All of it?

I begin slowly. "We have only half a box of stale crackers, jars of beans and tomatoes, and fish in the stream. We don't know where Pop is, and we don't have the money for rent. Or seed."

"Right." She seems almost pleased that I finally know what she's talking about. But she begins to cry again. "I didn't even have the money to run away."

That Cassie. I blow air through my lips.

"You sound like Xenia," she says.

"You don't sound as worried as you should be."

"It's because I told you. Now I don't have to worry about this by myself anymore."

My face is hot. I want to scream. Wait, I try to tell myself. Wait.

I know I love Cassie, but she's orange, as orange as a Halloween pumpkin.

CHAPTER TWENTY-TWO

I never get to make those cups of tea. Cassie and I go into the kitchen, and Joey takes a deep breath when he sees her. He looks down at the table. I know he's trying to remember that boys aren't supposed to cry.

He glances across at Anton, and the two of them grin at each other. Anton shrugs a little, gets up, and goes toward the back door.

I want to ask if he wants tea, but I'm so tired. "I will never forget this," I tell him, reminding me of my old self when I thought about words and how they sounded.

He nods and reaches for the doorknob.

"Wait a minute. What's that all over your hands?"

Anton looks down at them. "Paint, I guess."

And then he disappears up the lane.

The three of us go into the living room and fall onto the mattresses. Joey asks, "Where were you, Cassie?"

"In the barn."

"All that time?"

"Tell him the rest," I say. "Tell him that you've lost all our money."

Joey sits up, but Cassie is crying again.

I take pity on her. "We'll do something," I say, even though I can't imagine what it will be.

"All of it?" Joey says.

"I'm sorry," Cassie begins. And she goes through the whole story again.

I close my eyes. I have to think about that paint on Anton's hands, what I know it means, but it's so late and I need to sleep. Almost dreaming, I remember that old self of mine, writing letters, reading . . .

"She's not gone," I whisper, "not gone. . . ."

Morning comes fast. But I can't sleep anymore; I feel as if I'm in a fog.

Cassie's up ahead of me, sitting at the kitchen table.

"We'll just have to get help," she says. "We'll take ourselves down to the grocery store and—"

"Mr. Brancato isn't any better off than we are." Anger bursts in my chest. "The store is closed! Pop told us to find him at his house in case of an emergency. Do you know what *emergency* means?"

"No rent?" Cassie says. "No money?" She hesitates. "No food to feed Woodrow."

"No." I space the next words out as if I'm talking to someone who belongs on Pluto. "We will not go to Mr. Brancato." Pop's words come into my head. "I have to do this myself. No, not myself. Ourselves."

But then I stop. "Who's Woodrow?"

"My cat. Mine and Mr. Appleby's. Mr. Appleby gave me the food and I fed Woodrow every day." Cassie narrows her eyes at me. "Before you lost him." She sniffs. "Poor Woodrow. I still put food out for him, but maybe he's gone forever."

I can't believe it. "I fed him, too. Charlie the Butcher always gave me—" I break off. "I call him Clarence."

We stare at each other, and then I tell her about Miss Mitzi and her cat, Lazy, who came back. "We have to have hope."

I go outside and sit on the back step, staring at my garden, the damp dark earth ready to plant, and thinking about Clarence. Woodrow. Two meals a day.

But never mind that now. I have to find money. And pay the rent somehow.

I go back into the house and nearly step on one of the chickens. Gladys? I can't tell them apart anymore.

"What are we going to do, then?" Cassie says from the table. "Whatever—"

"Feed the chicks. Make yourself useful."

"Do I have to do everything?" she asks.

My mouth opens. "You're the one who lost all our money!"

But I've thought of one thing I can do first thing to-morrow morning. And just having an idea makes me feel a little better. *Look forward, Rachel,* I hear Mr. Appleby saying in my head.

CHAPTER TWENTY-THREE

It's rent day. I pull on my wrinkled Sunday dress and glance in the mirror. I must have grown when I wasn't looking. Either that or the dress shrank by itself. I grin a little.

My good shoes are under the bed. I pull them on; my feet have grown, too.

I run a comb through my hair, patting down the sides, until I'm sure I'm presentable.

Down in the kitchen, Cassie is sweeping the floor around the chickens. "Clean out a spot in the barn," I tell her. "And get them out there, if you don't mind."

She twitches one shoulder but she doesn't answer.

I glare at her. "Where's Joey?"

"He's up on the roof, polishing that rooster. He'll probably break his neck."

It's my turn not to answer. I know this about Joey now.

He does things that we think are dangerous. But he doesn't do anything he can't do. I really believe that. I go out the door and look up.

"Don't fall," I yell. "I'm going to town and I can't save you."

He waves down at me, that good egg Joey. "Don't worry. As soon as I finish this, I'm going fishing."

Along the road, the fields are green and the leaves on the trees overhead look new and washed. Things grow along the side of the road. I smell mint and see dandelions. I heard once you can make soup out of dandelions.

I talk to myself all the way to town, talk out loud, using the most persuasive voice I have. My hands are damp with worry. This has to work. Otherwise—

Never mind otherwise.

I stop to smooth down my hair once more, then turn in at the real estate office, listening to the jingle as I push open the door.

The real estate man sits with his feet up on the desk. He has nothing to do, I'm sure. Who's buying a farm now? Who's even renting?

He sees me and puts his feet down. "Hello?" he says; it's almost a question. He doesn't look overly friendly. A Miss Mitzi word, *overly*. I have a quick thought of her, sky-blue eyes, a white straw hat, and a pink rose in her lapel, when we all went to a museum last year.

"I want to talk to you about our farm," I say. "The one on Waltz Road."

There's a sign on his desk: MR. GRIMM. *Doesn't that just*

fit? Cassie would say. And because my knees are trembling, I slide into the seat across from him without asking.

He frowns. "I stopped by for the rent—"

I spread out my hands. "We don't have the money just yet." Every word is pulled out of me.

He raises his eyebrows.

"But we will!" I add.

"Listen, girlie, everyone tells me that. They say any day the money will come, someone is sending it." He leans forward. "The money never comes. They never pay."

"We'll pay," I say fiercely.

He blows air through thick lips. "I'll give you a week."

Seven days. How do I know Pop will send money by then? I don't, so I shake my head. "I need more time."

His eyebrows go up again. "Do you know what interest is?"

I don't know how to answer; I have no idea.

"It means that I'll give you more time, but you'll have to pay extra."

"How much time?"

"A month." He scribbles numbers on a piece of paper. "This much," he says.

"Fine." I barely look. The end of June, summer. I stand up. Who knows how much extra we'll pay? But I don't care.

A month. Thirty days.

CHAPTER TWENTY-FOUR

Outside, I sit on a bench facing the train station, the sun warm on my head. And then it comes to me: a great idea.

I stand up and find my way to the grain store. Inside, the man at the counter looks friendlier than Mr. Grimm. It's a good sign. "I'm an excellent worker," I say.

The feed man's lips twitch; he's trying not to laugh.

"I need a job."

He begins to shake his head.

"My goat ate my plants. I have to get seed."

His face changes. I can see he feels sorry for me.

"I could straighten your shelves," I tell him quickly.

What would Cassie say to that? I'm the sloppiest girl she knows.

"You could straighten that row of boxes, I guess. Put the seed packages where they belong. And in the next aisle, the nails are mixed up. You could sort them out. For seed. Not money."

"Yes." I nod. "That's what I want, just enough seed to plant my garden again."

Someone comes into the store, and the feed man waves me toward the aisle.

I spend the rest of the day working. It isn't as hard to be neat as I'd thought. But my shoes grow tighter as I move from one box to another, sorting nails, large, medium, or so small I wonder what they could possibly hold together. It's hard to concentrate on anything but my ankles rubbing against those too-small leather shoes.

"Closing time," the man says at last. He takes a while to check my work, neat stacks of pale brown bags labeled SUNFLOWERS, DAISIES, or BLUEBELLS, and separately, square white envelopes marked CUKES, TOMATOES, or about ten other vegetables.

"You can take five packets," he says. "Any five you want."

Choose wisely.

Whatever I grow will be what we eat. I long for corn on the cob, but Pop told me corn needed a whole field to make it turn out well.

I stand there in an agony of indecision. Miss Mitzi said that once about an arrangement she was putting together. Up in front, the feed man coughs a little; he wants to go home.

In a hurry, I choose squash and carrots and onions again. My fingers walk their way through the packs. Ah, beets and, at the last minute, lettuce.

"Good choices." He reaches back and takes out two more packs. "One is marigold seeds."

Marigolds!

He taps the other envelope. "I don't remember what these are. I forgot to label them." He shrugs. "Want them?"

"Sure." I duck my head. "I'm grateful."

He smiles. "I'm grateful, too. The shelves were a mess."

"Maybe I could help out again."

"Maybe," he says.

As soon as I'm away from the store, I pull off my shoes. I have blisters on both heels. But never mind. I clutch the small packets in my hands. A garden and thirty days to pay the rent.

It's late by the time I'm home. Cassie's waiting at the door. "I thought you were dead."

I stare at her, and her face reddens. We're both remembering her stay in the barn. I wave the packets at her and then at Joey, who comes to the door to see what's happening.

"Wow," Joey says when he hears about the rent and sees the seeds. Cassie breathes, "Oh, Rachel."

It's almost dark, but the three of us go outside and plant. We put the mystery seeds right in the middle. "Maybe it will be something really special," Cassie says.

We stand there grinning at each other, happy with ourselves.

"If only Pop could see this," Joey says.

"He'll see the best of it," Cassie says. "When it's all grown."

Cassie, surprising me.

CHAPTER TWENTY-FIVE

Today is perfect. I tell myself I'm going to have a holiday from worrying about the rent today.

Barefoot, I go out to look at our garden. Tiny green shoots cover the earth. I spot pale lettuce leaves; soon we'll have a taste. Leaning down, I brush my fingers over the mystery plants. What an odd smell they have.

Then I go to the barn and bring Xenia outside. She looks at the garden. "Oh, no!" I say. "Not this time."

Joey has put out a stake, and I tie her to it. There's enough room for her to move around, but our vegetables are safe!

Back in the barn, I pour some of her food into the pan and glance up at the painting of the girl reading. I look at her carefully. I can't see her face; she lies on her stomach, one ankle crossed over the other. She must be happy, because she's reading. Her book is painted blue.

I think of what my art teacher said: the painter always tries to tell you something.

What was he trying to tell me?

He. Not a girl.

Anton, with blue paint over his hands.

I give Xenia another pat, then go down to the stream.

I walk around the ferns and wade along the edge of the water until I reach the rock. And there's the painting: a girl in front of the school. I know that now because of the flagpole.

Something else about it makes me smile. I see now what the girl is wearing on her hands. Boxing gloves! The artist might have been laughing as he drew.

I turn and take the stream in the other direction, up toward the hills, toward Anton's cottage. It's a long way in bare feet, but I'm determined.

And at last I'm standing in front. "Hey, Anton," I yell.

Suppose his mother comes out, or his father. Nobody opens the door, but then there's a hand on my shoulder. I swivel around.

"You're going to wake the whole world," he says.

"How did you get into my house and paint all that stuff?"

"I did it before you came. No one was there. It was a great place to paint. Lots of walls." He hesitates. "I know I was mean that first night. I'd begun to think the house was mine, my own place to paint." He spreads his hands. "And then you moved in. Afterward, I was sorry I wasn't nicer."

I nod, thinking about my own meanness. "But you did

the one in the barn after that. And the one on the rock," I say.

"I wanted to see how long it would take for you to figure it out." Is he trying not to grin?

"I didn't make that mess in the school."

"That happened before you came. No one will blame you." Now he grins. "You were just stealing books."

"Borrowing." My stomach turns over. "I just meant to borrow." I picture my Rebecca book in the principal's office.

Anton's mother is at the door. It's the woman with the ferns I saw at the train station. She waves. "Want some breakfast?"

I shake my head; I don't want her to see how hungry I am.

At least—at the very least—I can stop worrying about being blamed for what happened in the school.

But what about *Rebecca?*

"At least muffins," the woman calls.

I can't resist. I stand at the door as she hands me three muffins in paper napkins.

Ah, one for each of us.

I head toward home, munching and looking up at that clear sky. Pluto is still up there, so far away, not worrying about rent or food. It must be cold, all those miles away from the sun.

How many miles away is Pop?

As I reach our house, I hear the sound of a motor. I stop. Could it be Mr. Grimm? I can feel the pulse in my throat, but then I take a breath. It's the mail truck.

The mailman reaches out, and I can see from here there's a letter.

A letter from Pop. How do I know it? I cross my fingers. I just do.

My dear children,

You can't imagine how much I miss you, or how worried I am for you. You must wonder why you haven't heard from me sooner. I've thought of that every day, worried over it. And you hear now only because Jeff Mills, one of the workers, is leaving—angry because we haven't been paid—and he'll mail our letters when he reaches the nearest town.

We are building that road across a mountain. As we dig, we hit rock very quickly, and that has to be blasted away. It's exhausting work; we move forward only a short distance at a time. But as we look back, we can see that new road, raw and almost yellow, growing behind us. How different it is from the banking that I know so well.

We've been promised our pay soon, but still it hasn't come. Every day I want to throw down my shovel as Jeff did and walk away, but suppose the money comes tomorrow or the next day? So I hold on, as I have to ask you to hold on, too. We'll be together someday soon, I promise.

Love,
Pop

CHAPTER TWENTY-SIX

For a long time I stand in the road, Pop's letter in my hand. He's alive, he's somewhere, and someday he'll be home. It just seems so long, though.

I look back to make sure Xenia is still where she's supposed to be. I see she's eaten a patch of weeds. She stares at me, almost as if she's saying, *Too bad for you, Rachel. I found something to eat anyway.*

I smile and go toward the back door. From the corner of my eye, I see something streak through the garden. I'm ready to go after it, but it's gone. And the letter from Pop is too exciting to bother about that right now. In the kitchen I put the letter on the table. Cassie and Joey read as we eat the muffins; Joey's is gone in a moment, but Cassie eats hers slowly, licking her fingers after every bite.

I go to the closet. Lined up neatly are the jars of beans, the tomatoes in juice. That's all there is. The beans are gray and my stomach turns as I look at them.

"I'll smother the beans in chives and dump tomatoes over the whole mess," Cassie says. "We'll hardly taste the beans."

Joey rolls his eyes. "Delicious."

I glance out the window, looking toward the garden. Is something moving in there?

Cassie is talking about going to town. "Days and days ago, when everything looked so terrible . . ."

Wait a minute. What is that out there, anyway?

My eyes fill. "Cassie. Look."

"Are you listening?" she asks.

"No. Come outside. Come quietly."

"You never pay attention," she says as she and Joey follow me outside. We stand on the step and I don't even have to point.

"Woodrow!" Cassie says, and she's crying, too.

"Clarence," I whisper. But who cares what his name is?

He's there, and he's safe, and he's rubbing his torn ear on the mystery plants.

"He's rubbing his face in catnip," Joey says. "Cats love it."

Catnip!

We go closer and the cat looks at us a little suspiciously.

"Don't you remember me?" Cassie bends down and puts her hand out.

Maybe he does remember, or maybe it's the catnip. But he lets her run her hand over his head.

I don't try. Maybe tomorrow. In the meantime, it's enough to see that he's gained a little weight. Poor mice, maybe, poor birds. But still, he's alive.

CHAPTER TWENTY-SEVEN

I go to sleep every night worrying about the rent. I dream about it and wake up thinking about it.

We eat those gray beans three times a day. We sit there staring at the ceiling so we don't have to look at them and holding our noses so we don't have to smell them. But even more important, we live on the fish Joey catches.

The sun is hot as I pat the plants in my garden. I have to thank the grain man for his generosity. I walk to the stream and plunk myself all the way down in the water, feeling the coolness of my soaked skirt against my legs.

I think about the house. How did it become so dear to me? Everything is wrong with it. No, not everything. It has a family now. I swallow. Almost a family. If only Pop were here. And Miss Mitzi, with her white straw hat and a rose pinned to her collar.

I crane my neck to look up at the willows, and spot a

house wren that has a huge song for such a small bird. How soothing to watch him, then to run my fingers through the ferns, which crowd each other now. Some of them have wide leaves; others are thin as knives. Which ones does Anton's mother send down to the florists in the city?

I wonder.

I stand and squeeze the water out of my hem. And then I splash through the stream toward Anton's.

I'm going to find out.

Dear Miss Mitzi,

I've discovered something. It's as good as the pot of gold at the end of a rainbow. Well, almost.

Anton's mother sells ferns to what she calls the ritzy flower shops in New York. She says this area is a gold mine of ferns, and that I can do it, too. She's going to tell me how.

I'm off to work at the grain store, for boxes and waxed paper. No time to write more.

I love you, Miss Mitzi.
Rachel

CHAPTER TWENTY-EIGHT

Cassie is painting. Everything in sight is turning gold. I'd like to tell her it was a mistake to let Xenia in for a visit. Gold hoofprints trot from one end of the hall to the other. For once, Cassie is furious at her. "That's it!" she says. "Back to the barn."

I go into the kitchen and pump water onto a rag. Back in the hall, I dab at the wet paint. Some of it comes up; some doesn't.

Cassie's staring at me. "Thanks, Rachel. Thanks."

I nod, surprised at myself, but glad about it.

She's on to something else. "We can't sleep in the living room anymore. It's a terrible habit, as if animals sleep there."

Joey and I grin at each other. We don't remind her that Xenia actually did sleep there. Instead, we drag the mattresses back upstairs, then the pillows.

But Cassie's not finished. The dust flies from one room to another, then out the door. And a day later she appears at breakfast with rag curlers poking out all over her head. "Clean yourselves up, please," she says. "We have to go to town today."

"Not me," Joey says.

"I tried to tell you two, but you didn't pay one bit of attention."

Joey supplies fish for Clarence-Woodrow every day. The cat is still mean, but he's ours, and I love him even though his disposition is appalling.

I love that word.

Cassie points a fork at us. "You won't be sorry."

I'll be sorry; I know it. That long walk to town. No shoes that fit. "What are you talking about?"

"I will never ask you to do one more thing for the rest of your lives." And then she says something strange. "I know you said we should do everything on our own—"

"And we are, almost," I say.

"But I thought you were wrong. I thought we needed help."

Impossible. Who knows what she's talking about?

"All right, we'll go with you," I say.

Joey looks at the ceiling. "I guess."

She pulls at one of her curlers, then goes upstairs to find something else to clean or paint.

Joey shrugs at me.

After lunch, we wend our way to town. When Pop gets home, we'll take the truck. I'll never walk so far again for the rest of my life.

In front of me Cassie's curls are enormous, sticking out all over her head. She plunks herself down on the bench in front of the real estate office.

I spent yesterday afternoon at the grain store. I traded three hours of work for boxes and paper. Anton's mother, Mrs. Freeman, is going to show me how to cut the ferns and send them. She's also going to lend me the money for postage.

I didn't want her to do that, but she said it was no bother, none at all.

I sit on the bench next to Cassie, my eyes closing against the sun and against Mr. Grimm, who is sitting in the window two inches away from me. "What are we doing here?" I ask Cassie, hardly moving my lips.

"I know you said I couldn't ask the grocery man for help, but I had to do something."

I stare at her.

"We were eating beans," she said.

"There were wild strawberries."

"And I've been fishing," Joey says.

She doesn't answer.

Across the way a train steams into the station. Soot and cinders fly everywhere. Cassie shouts over the noise. "I thought I had to save us."

What is she talking about?

A hobo scurries across the street, ready to jump on the train. Cassie is still shouting, even though the train has stopped. "I wrote a letter. I brought it to the post office myself. I used my life savings." She grins a little. "Two cents."

I put my hand up to my face. When I see who's getting off the train, I begin to cry and I don't even try to stop.

Because coming toward us, wearing her best Sunday dress and the blue cloche that matches her eyes, is Miss Mitzi Madden.

"I told her we were in despair over food," Cassie says. "I didn't mention the rent. One problem is enough."

Despair!

Imagine Cassie using such a word.

Miss Mitzi holds out her arms, and somehow there's room enough for the three of us. And Miss Mitzi is talking, talking. . . . "I had to get someone to take care of the store. And when that didn't work out, I stamped my feet, locked the door, and wrote to Cassie to say, 'Hold your horses, I'm on my way.'" She grins at us. "And here I am."

By this time she's out of breath, so we hug again, all of us laughing.

SUMMER

CHAPTER TWENTY-NINE

It's the first day of summer. We've dragged Miss Mitzi from one end of the farm to the other. She loves it, all of it, even Xenia, who tried to eat the hem of her skirt.

We've had wonderful meals. Miss Mitzi pulled tons of food from her suitcase, and then we walked to the store, and she bought more. Cassie cooks and cooks.

"This place is truly lovely," Miss Mitzi keeps saying. "Look at all you've done by yourselves. Rachel's garden, Cassie's painting, Joey's rooster."

There's a syrupy feeling in my chest. Miss Mitzi always knows the perfect things to say.

Cassie found an old dress for her in the closet, a work dress. Today we go over to Anton's to help as Mrs. Freeman shows us how to send the ferns down to New York.

Miss Mitzi loves the ferns. "Maybe you'll sell me a few to take back to my flower shop," she says.

As if we wouldn't give her everything we have!

But what we try to do is keep her with us. We try everything.

Joey spends the afternoons fishing; Miss Mitzi says they're the best fish she's ever tasted. She even likes the tomatoes and beans that Cassie throws in with Miss Mitzi's vegetables.

"And we have plenty of beans," Cassie says, grinning.

Cassie with a sense of humor! Now that Miss Mitzi is here, she's not as orange as she used to be.

Cassie has given her gold room to Miss Mitzi. "You can stay here forever," she says.

But Miss Mitzi shakes her head a little and puts her hand on Cassie's shoulder.

One day, in my garden, Miss Mitzi bends down and crumbles the rich earth in her fingers. "Gorgeous."

She waves at Clarence, who is sitting on a rock at the stream. Clarence pretends that he doesn't see her, or any of us.

I keep telling her how much we want her here. "We'll eat from the garden all summer. We'll splash in the stream." I don't mention rent. Miss Mitzi would give us all her money; I know that. But I can't let her do that. I'm sure she doesn't have much.

Her sky-blue eyes are so sad I have to look away. But my words tumble out. "Xenia will give us milk someday. We'll have a rooster, and the chickens will give us eggs."

Still she doesn't answer.

I put my arms around her. "You love your shop? You can't bear to leave it?"

Her face is fierce. "Do you think I'd care about that shop for one minute if I could have all of you?"

"Well, then."

"Your father . . ." She almost breathes it.

"He cares about you, Miss Mitzi, I know he does."

She shakes her head. "I don't know it. Not one bit. He's never really said . . ."

"But if he had said . . ."

"Ah, Rachel. Wouldn't it be heaven to be here? To look up every morning and see Joey's golden rooster? To gather ferns?"

I'm hardly listening. I keep hearing her say *He's never really said*.

"Wait," I say. "Just wait."

Inside, I take the stairs two at a time and open Pop's door. It's been weeks since I've been in there, but it's still the same: Miss Mitzi's picture on the dresser, Pop's letter to her under the doily.

I close my eyes. What might happen, what could happen, what will happen next?

Then I take the picture and the letter downstairs to show Miss Mitzi.

CHAPTER THIRTY

When Miss Mitzi takes the train back to the city, we wave until we can't see her blue cloche in the window anymore.

By the time we get back to the house, it's late afternoon. In the mailbox are two letters. One is from Bensen's Florists, Park Avenue, New York City. It has the fern money, not enough to pay every bit of the rent and the interest, but much more than half. They write that they want more ferns to use in their arrangements.

We're getting there. Somehow, the real estate man will just have to give us a few more days. I may have to beg.

But, ah, the next letter is from Pop. Dollar bills with their large gold seals fall out of the envelope, enough for Mr. Grimm! And the greatest news. Pop will be home in days. *Watch for me*, he writes. *You'll see me coming up over the hill.*

Cassie and I dance around Joey, laughing and crying

at the same time. Through my blurred eyes, I see tears on Joey's cheeks. "We've done it," I say.

"With a little help," Cassie says.

"The house is ours," I say. "This beautiful falling-apart house. We'll pay Mr. Grimm on time." And we begin to laugh again and the three of us are holding hands.

"But isn't Pop in trouble?" Cassie says with glee in her voice.

That was the biggest surprise of Miss Mitzi's visit. "Hmmpf," she said when she read the letter. She narrowed her eyes. "He could have saved me all this sadness. Wouldn't you think he'd have told me that he wanted me to come? Wouldn't you think he would have let me decide whether I wanted to take a chance on this old place?"

She smiled at us. "You know what I would have said."

The next day, she threw her clothes into her suitcase. She jammed her blue cloche over her dark curls.

"You're leaving?" we asked, the three of us at once.

"Don't go back to the city!" I said.

"Please . . . ," Cassie said.

"Don't worry," said Miss Mitzi. "I'm just going to close up the shop and pack my things. Business has been terrible, anyway. I'll be back here by the time your father gets home, to give him a piece of my mind."

The three of us let out our breath.

"And . . ." She holds up one finger and gives us her light-up-the-world smile. "If all else fails, I can always sleep in the barn with Xenia."

* * *

We've eaten our way through the jars of green beans. There's only one left. We hear someone whistle.

"Is that—" Joey jumps up.

"Pop." Cassie picks up the last jar and tosses it out the back door. "I will never eat beans again."

Pop!

I'm out the door ahead of the other two, around the side of the house to the front. Pop is coming up the front path. He looks worn and tired, much thinner than when he left, but his smile is huge.

We meet halfway, all of us with our arms out.

"Home," he says, holding us.

Inside, we talk, one louder than the other. Everyone has something to say.

And then we get to the Miss Mitzi part. We tell Pop what we think, what Miss Mitzi thinks.

And he says he thinks exactly the way we all do.

Dear Miss Mitzi,

This is the last time I will ever write to you. I don't even have to mail it, because you'll be here this afternoon. I'll just leave it on the table for you.

It's certainly the last time I'll ever call you Miss Mitzi, because once you and Pop are married next Saturday, everything will be different.

In the meantime, I went to the goat lady, who is also the teacher. I told her every single bit about the books. She walked me back to the school and let me borrow three books. Three. (I lent her my Rebecca book. She said she'd love to read it again.)

She's keeping her fingers crossed that school will begin again this fall.

Things are really looking up. Pop is going to work part-time at the bank. You and I will write letters to the rest of the world, and garden, and fix the house.

And we'll sell ferns . . . millions of ferns.

I must tell you, I will never forget Colfax Street, but everything I truly love will be here now. Cassie and Joey. Pop. School, maybe. And even Clarence. We'll never know how Clarence survived the winter, but he's—what's that word?—resourceful. Yes, he's a resourceful guy, that cat. He likes to do things on his own.

I keep saying to myself, Miss Mitzi will be our new mother.

It's gratifying, all of it.

Simply gratifying.

All my love,
Rachel

PATRICIA REILLY GIFF is the author of many beloved books for children, including the Kids of the Polk Street School books, the Friends and Amigos books, and the Polka Dot Private Eye books. Several of her novels for older readers have been chosen as ALA-ALSC Notable Children's Books and ALA-YALSA Best Books for Young Adults. They include *The Gift of the Pirate Queen; All the Way Home; Water Street; Nory Ryan's Song*, a Society of Children's Book Writers and Illustrators Golden Kite Honor Book for Fiction; and the Newbery Honor Books *Lily's Crossing* and *Pictures of Hollis Woods*. *Lily's Crossing* was also chosen as a *Boston Globe–Horn Book* Honor Book. Her books for younger readers in the Zigzag Kids series are *Number One Kid, Big Whopper, Flying Feet*, and *Star Time*. Her most recent books for older readers include *Storyteller, Wild Girl*, and *Eleven*. Patricia Reilly Giff lives in Connecticut.

Visit her on the Web at PatriciaReillyGiff.com.